Wondrous Journeys in Strange Lands

Wondrous Journeys in Strange Lands

Sonia Nimr

translated by
Marcia Lynx Qualey

Interlink Books

An imprint of Interlink Publishing Group, Inc.
Northampton, Massachusetts

First published in 2021 by

Interlink Books
An imprint of
Interlink Publishing Group, Inc.
46 Crosby Street
Northampton, Massachusetts 01060
www.interlinkbooks.com

Originally published in Arabic by Tamer Institute-Ramallah-Palestine, 2013
Cover images: Abstract colorful bird © Epifantsev | Dreamstime.com;
Antique Vintage Leather Book Cover © Heike Falkenberg | Dreamstime.com

Library of Congress Cataloging-in-Publication Data available
ISBN 978-1-62371-866-4

Printed and bound in the United States of America

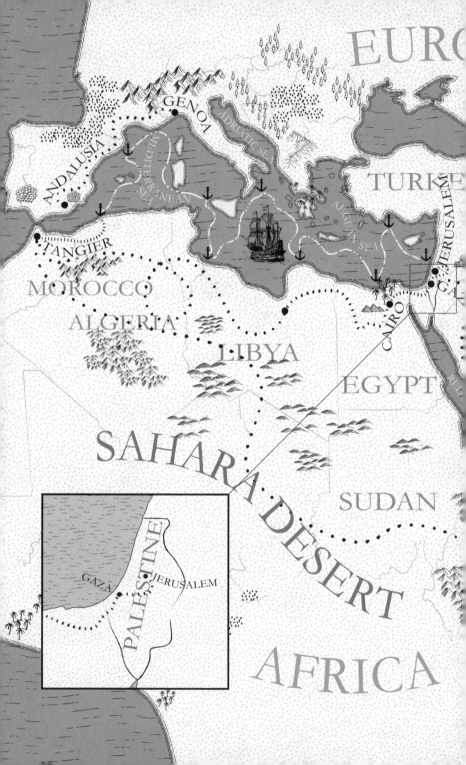

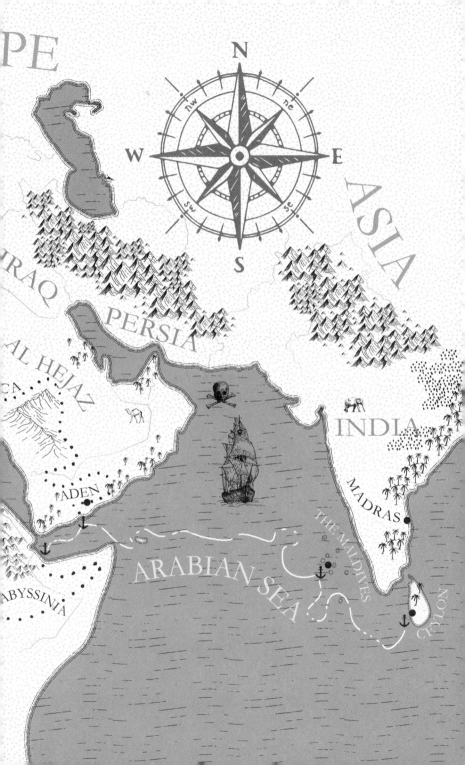

PROLOGUE

When I received an invitation to attend a conference in Morocco, I nearly soared with joy. It had been one of my dearest wishes to visit this country that was so rich in civilization and culture. And yet I didn't know that this would set off an adventure that would change the course of my life, or that destiny would put in my hands these notes on the life of an unknown woman.

To begin at the beginning.

After a series of long and complicated travel preparations, I arrived in beautiful Marrakesh, and everything was going smoothly. The conference was interesting, and I had the opportunity to meet a number of specialists in the field of Islamic art, and to see its artisans' creations. When I stepped down from the podium after my talk, one of the participants greeted me warmly. He was dark-skinned, with North African features, short and very thin, carrying an overstuffed leather briefcase that looked to be heavier than him. He told me his name was Professor Ahmadi, an emeritus of the University of Rabat, now living in Tangier and writing about Islamic art.

Following this introduction and exchange of pleasantries, Professor Ahmadi asked if he could invite me to have a cup of coffee with him in the lobby of the hotel where the conference was taking place, saying he had something he wished to share with me.

We drank our coffee and chatted for a while, and then he removed the coffee cups that sat in front of us, pushed away the ashtray, drank the rest of his water and placed the glass on a nearby table. He performed all of these actions extremely slowly, as though he were practicing a ritual or procrastinating to buy time before he began to speak. This increased my curiosity, and questions began to weigh heavily on my mind. The professor cleared his throat. Without introduction, he spoke in an academic manner.

"It was approximately six months ago when a man approached me, saying he had purchased a home by the sea, and, while making repairs, had discovered a jar buried in the sands beneath the house. He thought this was a treasure and opened it, but instead found a bundle of papers, carefully bound in silken thread. The man did not understand the contents of these papers, and thus brought them to me."

The professor did not look up at my face to see the effect of his words, but rather bent down to pick up his leather briefcase, which he placed on his lap. Once he'd opened it with great deliberateness, he looked up to gauge my expression, which had shifted from curiosity to astonishment to intense excitement. He put his hand into the bag and took out a thick brown envelope that he set on the table before placing his bag back beside him on the floor. Then he reached into the envelope.

"I came to realize that the author of these papers came from Palestine, your homeland."

Now I was very eager! The whole subject was thrilling, and I couldn't stop my hands from inching across the table and stroking the back of the envelope. I asked myself: *What's in these papers? How did they reach Tangier, thousands of miles from Palestine? What secrets do they hide within them?*

The professor pushed the envelope toward me, saying, "I hesitated a great deal before giving this to you, as it's rare for researchers such as us to find an opportunity like this. I intended to work on this manuscript myself. But as you can see I've grown old, and I feared something might happen to me and the papers might be lost, or that they would perhaps not find someone to cherish them after I was gone."

Having said that, he reached into his shirt pocket and took out a card, which he handed to me.

"Please write to me. I will be curious to know your opinion."

He extended his hand once again, over the envelope, as though he wanted to bid it farewell. Then he looked at his watch and stood up.

"It's nearly time for the session at which I will speak. Take good care of these papers, and I wish you success."

He picked up his empty briefcase and walked quickly to the hall, as if he were afraid of turning back and seizing the papers. As for me, I remained where I was, stunned, staring at the envelope and holding it without finding the courage to look inside.

I ordered another cup of coffee and began to slowly open the envelope, as though I were afraid the contents might leap out of my hands. The papers inside were stacks of yellowed rectangles, each carefully arranged and wrapped in rolls, and each roll bound with a pink thread. I opened the first parcel and found it adorned with elegant penmanship in small letters, its characters beautiful and harmonious. At the bottom of the last page was a signature.

Ajeeba

I began to read, my heart racing as my eyes slid over the lines.

1

1
THE CURSE

And so it was that my mother went into labor while sitting astride the donkey that was carrying her from the city to our village. My father had to halt the caravan and pitch a small tent at the foot of the mountain. In that long-ago tent, my mother bore twins: my sister Shams, or "Sun," and me, Qamar, or "Moon."

It was a difficult birth. If it weren't for the quick-wittedness of our servant, Aisha, and the instructions my mother gave despite her condition, she would have died bringing my sister and me into the world. For seven days, she stayed in that tent at the foot of the mountain, before managing to continue on the hardest part of their journey: the climb up the mountain.

That summer was searing hot, and travel was almost suicide. But it was the only time of year when the wide valley surrounding the mountain could safely be crossed by those who wanted to reach our village. My father had left his nameless village in the north of Palestine nearly four years before, thinking he would never return. Yet fate had other plans.

My father's village was a tiny, remote hamlet perched high on the mountain, and its people lived by farming and sheep herding. Once each year, the men of the village went down the mountain to the city, traveling on foot or by donkey for two days to reach it. There, they would sell their produce of cheese, fruit, and olives, and their leather hides, and they would buy what they needed of clothes, tools, and sometimes even books. In the city, the men would also learn news of the past year, like the name of their country's latest ruler, and other talk. Since only the adult men from our village went down to the city, none of the women knew what this city looked like, or how to reach it.

"The Village," as the people who lived there called it, was so isolated that no one knew of its existence, except for a few of the merchants who traded with the villagers. No one ever visited there. The men made their journey in the summer, when the wide valley surrounding the mountain dried out. For the rest of the year, the village was isolated by the waters that filled the valley below.

All the people in the village were relatives, born of one original family. The story went like this.

Sheikh Saad, the village's first elder, had fled the south of Palestine hundreds of years ago. He had murdered a man, and he feared revenge from the man's family. So, Sheikh Saad wandered with his family for a long time, until he had a dream. In it he saw an enormous tree with leaves that were always green, throwing their broad shade over a mountain. So, he traveled north, searching until he found that tree. There, on the mountain, he built his house—and the village.

Over the years, the village established its own laws and beliefs, created and enforced by the Council of Elders. The villagers believed that if anyone left there to live somewhere far away, it would bring a curse onto the village, dragging misfortune and ruin in its wake. They also believed that, if a stranger were to come into the village, they would bring catastrophe, perhaps leaving them cursed for all time. So, marriage to men outside the village was forbidden—although, since women weren't allowed to leave, marriage to an outsider was impossible anyway!

In the village, only boys were allowed to learn to read. Girls were barred from education and denied books for fear that books would corrupt them.

Life in the village went on like this for many years. Laws took root and grew more and more complex, such that no one even dared to think of staying in the city for more than the two sanctioned weeks. Certainly, no one dared marry outside the village. Neither did the women think of learning, nor did the girls think of playing. And no one dared raise their eyes to meet the gazes of the village's long-bearded elders, who were its absolute rulers. If one of the elders passed by on the road, the men would stop working. They would look down, staring at the ground until the elder had passed.

As for the women, whether they worked out in the fields or stayed at home, they were not allowed to take a single honest look at the elders, but instead had to be satisfied—or even happy—that the only reason they might be allowed in the elders' presence was during an appearance before the court. That was where they would end up if their husband filed a complaint against them. In these cases, the elders' rulings were harsh. Either they would order that the woman be beaten in the village square, or they'd order her to be locked up in a house with other guilty wives. The woman might stay there for several months, depending on the severity of the accusation.

The House of Shamed Wives was a small, one-room shack at the edge of the village, with neither windows nor light. There, a woman would live on dry bread and water until the end of her sentence. Then, she'd have to promise not to raise her head in front of her husband, nor speak to him, unless she had been spoken to first.

And yet, despite all the strict laws and extreme caution, a curse befell the village.

One day, a man named Suleiman fled the village and did not return. The men of the village said that Suleiman loved a girl from the city who, they claimed, was a *jinn*. It was she who had possessed his mind and made him commit this crime. The curse began with his departure, and the Village Elders could do nothing about it.

It was a great and disastrous curse. For fifty years, the village women gave birth only to male children. Even the sheep gave birth only to males. And, as the youngest woman in the village grew older and older, fear crept into the men's hearts. The population of women dwindled, and men began to shake their heads when they learned that their wives had given birth to a boy. The elders forbade the traditional celebrations for a male birth. The women craved girls, and they had their boys wear girls' clothes and grow out their hair.

Despite many attempts, the healers failed to discover a solution, and all the special prayers did not help. No, despite all the sacrifices of slaughtered calves, the curse still hung over the village. And yet, even with this disaster, the Council of Elders still forbade men from marrying outside the village, believing that if they could catch Suleiman the fugitive and offer him as a sacrifice, the curse would be lifted. His family continued to search for him. But what none of them knew was that, just a few months after he'd arrived in the city, Suleiman had died of a mysterious illness.

My father, Saeed, was the youngest boy in the village. When boys reached the age of thirteen, it was the men's custom each year to take them to the city as an initiation into manhood. So, my father Saeed went with his father, his uncle, and the rest of the village men down the mountain. And from the moment my father saw the city, he couldn't stop thinking about it!

The first thing that struck him was its size. Then he was dazzled by its colors, since the village was dominated by shades of brown and black in all their variations, if it was even possible to vary them. The elders had long forbidden the use of bright colors as too flashy and extravagant, and they had imposed brown and black as a sign of pious modesty. But in the city, colors danced before Saeed's eyes in the shimmering sun: reds, greens, pinks, yellows, blues, and golds. And then there was the market! Never before in his life had he seen so many people and shops—for clothing and wares and scents and books! The men stayed in the khan. The khan was itself a wonder: a huge, two-floor rectangular building, with an enormous yard in the middle. Travelers would shelter their animals downstairs, and the khan's attendants would take care of them, while the travelers lodged in the rooms upstairs. There were also many shops and craft corners in and around the yard. For Saeed, the khan contained a whole world within its walls.

In the city he saw shops that specialized in selling books, and he was amazed to see so many of them together in one place. Compared to this, even the village library looked like a single shelf. There were books on shelves, books on the floor, books in boxes stacked one on top of another—a mountain of books!

When they arrived at the market, Saeed asked his father for permission to buy books. His father explained that no one was allowed to buy books that hadn't been selected by the Council of Elders. Anyone found with a book that wasn't approved by the Council would face a heavy penalty. Saeed stood in front of the bookshops, in dazed surprise, wishing he could stay there for a hundred years so he could read all these masterpieces.

He snuck into one shop and glanced around. There, he found a book with a reddish cover, emblazoned with the image of a colorful bird. Written on the cover in beautiful calligraphy was the title: *Wondrous Journeys in Strange Lands.* He opened it and began to flip through the pages. On every page, he discovered colorful images, maps, and the names of cities and countries of which he had never heard. Pictures of birds and animals seared his imagination.

My father stood for a long time, contemplating the book's pictures and its beautiful form, without noticing that the shop owner was watching him. Suddenly, he was startled by the man's voice, asking if he'd like to buy this book. Saeed apologized and returned the book to its place without shifting his gaze. When the shopkeeper tried to tempt him to buy it, Saeed explained that he couldn't bring it to his village. The shopkeeper realized that my father came from "that village" and invited him to visit every day during his stay, so he could read as many books as possible.

The next day, the village men dispersed. Some went to exchange goods, while others went to search for a doctor, a magician, or even a sorcerer to help lift the village curse. The rest split up to seek out news of Suleiman, meeting each evening at the khan

This gave Saeed a golden chance, and he hurried to the bookshop. It was open, but he stopped when he saw no sign of the shopkeeper. Then he heard a soft voice, asking if he was in search of a particular book. Saeed looked up. There was a girl his age, lovely and slender, as if she were from a dream. She said she was the daughter of the bookshop owner, who had gone to pray at the mosque, and she was watching the store until he returned.

Saeed stood in front of her without understanding a thing the girl said. He was stunned and sweaty. Never in his life had he seen a girl like her—well, no! Never in his life had he seen *any girl at all*. His mother was the youngest woman in the village. What's more, the village's women covered their whole bodies. Even their heads were swathed in black wraps, while this girl had a bare face and head. She said her name was Jawaher and that she loved books. Saeed was stunned by this wonder of wonders—women who were not forbidden to read!

He asked if she had read all the books in the shop, and she laughed and said she'd tried. She gestured to the book with the red cover, saying it was her favorite, and that she loved it because it transported her to distant lands and new cities, to people of different colors and shapes and customs.

Saeed sat on the floor and listened to Jawaher talk about the book and about her wish to travel someday to all these lands and places. Saeed's nerves calmed a little, and he began to shower her with questions about the city, and the life there, and whether there were public places to bathe, and whether the ruling prince was really married to ten women—a thousand and one questions. Jawaher asked him about his village and its people, its customs and laws.

The two weeks passed in the blink of an eye, and Saeed came to say goodbye to the bookshop owner and his daughter. As he walked away from them, heartsick, Jawaher called out. She came to him and handed him the book *Wondrous Journeys,* saying it was a gift. He couldn't refuse, so he hid the book in the folds of his clothes. He knew he would never forget this visit, and it would remain forever printed on his mind and heart. As he hurried away, he touched the book—the book that would bring him and my mother together once more, and the only book I would carry with me when I left his village forever.

The men returned from the city laden with goods, tools, and clothes. They were also laden with disappointment, as they'd failed to discover anything about Suleiman, or to find a way to lift the village curse.

But as for Saeed, he had left his heart and mind in the city, and he returned with a magical book in the folds of his clothes. From that moment, he was seized with an obsessive desire to return both to the city and to Jawaher, who had captured his imagination and filled the whole of his being with love.

And so, my father decided to leave the village for the city. What he didn't know was that his departure would be the cause of a journey full of obstacles and misery. Nor did he know that his journey would end in the very village he'd left.

Seven years passed, and he turned twenty. At last, he was old enough to return to the city alongside the men, with the red book back in the folds of his clothes and a plan lodged in his mind. His heart raced ahead of him to the city, while his feet stopped when he reached the front of the bookshop.

Jawaher greeted him, and his heart froze. She had grown into a beautiful woman! He stood in front of her, as beaded with sweat as he had been at their first meeting. Then he sat down to resume their conversation, as though it had not been years since he was last here. He took the book out from his clothes to return it, but she refused—it was a gift.

Saeed told the bookshop owner about his plan to stay in the city, and the man welcomed it, offering Saeed a job working alongside him, selling books. And with that, Saeed disappeared.

When Saeed didn't return, the men of the village searched for him. They even delayed their return by two days, but without success. Some thought there might have been an accident, but others believed he had fled, like Suleiman. They didn't dare speak these thoughts aloud. After all, Saeed was the grandson of the head of the Elders' Council, and he couldn't possibly have dreamt of running away!

While the men, filled with disappointment and fear of the Elders' anger, returned to the village without Saeed, Saeed himself began work in the bookshop. It was a job he enjoyed very much. At times, when the bustle of the market subsided and there were only a few customers in the shop, he would sit reading in a corner or discussing events or a book with Jawaher and her father. Their words were a marvel to him: their knowledge, their broad horizons, and their wisdom.

It wasn't long before Saeed married Jawaher. For a time, the two of them lived in happiness and comfort. When Jawaher's father died, she and Saeed continued to run the bookshop together. Meanwhile, the people of the village lived in terror those three years. Because of Saeed's disappearance, they were afraid of some new disaster or greater curse, and they searched for him every time they went down to the city.

My mother was in the final months of pregnancy when it happened. By chance, my father ran into Omar, his childhood friend and companion. For most of the two weeks that the villagers were in the city, my father stayed out of sight. But then my mother was struck by severe stomach pains, such that my father had to go to the apothecary to bring her herbal remedies. And there was Omar, buying medicines. Saeed took him by the hand and led him to the bookshop, where he pulled Omar behind a curtain. Saeed wouldn't let Omar leave until he'd promised not to breathe one word to the people of the village.

My father learned from Omar that his father, my grandfather, had died the year before, and that the curse was still in force. He learned that the people still blamed Suleiman until that very hour, while Saeed's name had fallen into total silence. People were banned from speaking his name or relating his story. It was as though he'd never been.

My father was deeply hurt by this, but he forgave the people of the village. Then he learned that his mother was very sick. Despite the ban, *she* repeated his name, day and night. He wished that he could see her, if for only a moment, before she died.

So, he decided to return to the village. My father sold what could be sold and carried the rest, loading their furniture and most of the books from the shop onto a caravan of donkeys. And together my father and mother left for the village.

2
THE STRANGER

The news that my father was headed back to the village arrived even before he'd reached the foot of the mountain. When he arrived with my exhausted mother and the caravan of donkeys carrying the books and furniture, the village was completely empty, as if its people had suddenly disappeared. In the narrow, dusty streets, there was not even a chicken or a stray dog. He arrived at my grandfather's house and knocked on the door, calling out, "It's me, Mama, it's Saeed. I've come back!"

But my grandmother, who wept behind the door when she heard my father's voice, didn't open it for him. He knocked a second time, and a third, calling out to her. But the door didn't open, and her sobs behind it grew louder.

My father went back down the streets of the silent village, as the hot wind blew dust and dirt into his eyes. He stood in the village square and shouted, "Is anyone here?" The only answer was silence and dust.

That's when my father understood that the villagers considered him dead. No one would speak to him, or open a door to let him in.

He took his sad caravan to the far edge of the village, where the olive trees stood. There, he set up camp. So, it was decided that we would live in a tent beside this village where silence and isolation were the rule. And after several months of continuous labor, my father finished building a small wooden house where our family could live.

For the whole of this time, no one spoke to either my mother or my father. The villagers became like ghosts, disappearing the moment either of them were spotted. Brown-skinned Aisha, my mother's trustworthy maid, was the only one who could break this blockade. One moonless night, she went to my grandmother's house. My grandmother trembled in fear as she opened the door. She turned off the lamp and closed the curtains, then lit a candle that she sheltered in her shaking hands.

If the people of the village were to learn of this visit, my grandmother would die alone, with no one to attend her funeral or to pray for her in the mosque. My grandmother was afraid to die alone. This fear was as great as her love for my father, as great as her desire to hear his news.

Brave Aisha told her news of my father, and of his twin children. She described our beauty for my grandmother: "One is blonde and pale as snow, just like her grandmother." When she heard this, my grandmother smiled for the first time. "We call her Shams, after the Sun," Aisha said. "And the second is brown-skinned, with hair like the night, after her mother. She has a lock of white hair above her forehead, like a full moon in the deepest of darkness. We call her Qamar, after the Moon."

My grandmother longed to see her granddaughters, to hold us, play with us, and sing songs to us. But all she got was Aisha's description. And while she wanted to hear more, she told Aisha, "Go now, before the dawn comes and someone sees you. Tell my son I forgive him in this world and the next. Tell him I'll die, but that I'm happy for him, and my heart calls out to him day and night. And tell his wife, the stranger, to be patient."

The next morning, the villagers found my grandmother dead in her bed, with a radiant smile on her face. It was as though God had stretched out her life just long enough to hear news of her son, and now there was no longer a reason to prolong her sufferings.

My father walked far behind the funeral. He was present and absent, there and not there, as he followed my grandmother's journey to her final resting place. The people of the village saw him with tears streaming down his face, but they paid him no attention and didn't approach him to offer their condolences. After they'd thrown dirt over my grandmother and read verses from the Quran, they returned to the village in silence.

When my father was sure these ghosts had left the cemetery, and the last of them had disappeared behind the trees, he threw himself on Grandmother's grave, weeping and throwing dirt on himself. He stayed like that until my mother came and pulled him away with gentle hands.

During the olive season, when my sister Shams and I were five years old, we stood watching the faraway workers from in front of our house. The men and women did their olive picking in silence. In the evenings they left, their bags of olives borne by donkeys. Not one of them spoke to us or even looked at us, even though Shams and I called out and waved to them. And when the villagers had finished picking the olives, a circle of trees around our house remained untouched. Those trees, we tended.

After we had finished picking our olives, I asked my father, "Baba, aren't there any children in the village?"

My father gave a sad smile and gently placed me on his knee.

"There were children in the village. But they turned into angels and went back to heaven."

"Did they go back to heaven because no one talked to them?"

I could see tears on my father's cheeks, and he looked at my mother as though pleading with her. My mother stopped pounding the olives with her round stone and sighed loudly, and I heard Aisha say, "There is no power and strength except in God."

My mother's tone was tough but affectionate.

"Aren't you going to help your sister and I pound these olives?"

But again, I asked my father, "Are Shams and I going to turn into angels and go to heaven like the kids from the village?"

"No, sweetheart," he said, lifting Shams onto his other knee and pulling us against his chest. "You're the ones who'll bring the children back to the village someday."

Then he lifted us off his knees and stood up.

"But now I must bring the firewood, or we won't eat tonight."

"But how can we bring children back to the village?" I insisted.

He smiled softly. "One day, you'll find a way. For now, help your mother."

We were eating dinner when we heard a light knock at the door. We stopped eating. None of us dared to move.

"Who would come when we haven't had a visit in all these years?" Aisha asked, moving her massive body toward the door. We turned our gazes toward the door, the question twitching on all our lips.

Aisha returned, followed by a woman wearing a black robe that covered her body from head to toe. She held part of the robe in her hand, lifting it up to cover her face. She spoke suddenly, in an emotional voice.

"If the villagers knew I came here, they'd kill me. But I couldn't find another way, I just couldn't find any other way…"

And she began, faintly, to cry.

My mother stood and put her hand on the woman's shoulder, which shuddered at her touch. My mother asked her to sit, but the woman refused, speaking between sobs.

"My son—my son, he's sick, please! My only son… Everyone says you're a witch, and whoever comes near you will die. But I don't care about death, I don't care if I die. I just want to save my son. Please, use your magic to save him!"

As the woman spoke, she sank to the ground, trying to kiss my mother's feet. My mother lifted her up and asked her, calmly, "What's the matter with your son?"

"It's the fever."

The woman wiped her tears with the edge of her black cloak, and we saw her exhausted eyes.

"He has the shakes and the sweats. Sometimes he mutters things I can't understand, and then he passes out. He's going to die. Please…save him!"

The woman tried again to kiss my mother's feet. My mother asked Aisha to bring some water and then said to the woman, "Wait here." She left the room briefly and returned with a book, flipping through its pages.

"Is he vomiting?"

"Yes, but he hasn't eaten anything in days. He's going to die…" And the woman went on wailing.

My mother left the room again, and Aisha embraced the woman, pulling her to her chest.

"Don't be afraid. She will find a solution. Don't be afraid."

"But if they knew I came, they'd kill me!" the woman said in a trembling voice.

"No one's going to die," Aisha said. "Calm down and trust God."

My mother returned with a bunch of herbs and offered them to the woman, telling her to boil them and give the liquid to her sick son three times a day. The woman took the herbs and stood, hesitating. My mother gave her a questioning smile.

"But aren't you going to kill me?" the woman asked. "I mean, well…"

"Not today. I am refraining from killing for two months," my mother reassured her gently.

"Thank you, you're a good witch!" the woman said, and she ran out.

In our house, the book room was my favorite place, and the favorite place of my sister Shams, too. Our father built shelves into the walls, and he and my mother carefully arranged the books. It was the quietest room in the house, and I loved to sit in there, breathing in the scent of paper that hung in the room. It was a smell I never found anywhere else. I've held it in my memory and searched for it the rest of my life: a smell like musk mixed with scented herbs, infused with a smell of something old I could neither name nor describe. The smells are still here, in my memory, and yet I can never quite conjure them up.

Shams and I would flip through the books and look at the pictures, imagining ourselves as colorful birds of paradise, or on Noah's Ark, as wild mares. The pictures gave us endless fodder for our imaginations, and ideas for inventing lots of games.

My mother never asked us to leave the book room, despite how much she cared for it. She encouraged us to browse the books, and she would read to us for almost an hour every day. She took charge of our education, and her lessons were strict. She taught us our alphabet and numbers, and how to hold a quill and form our first letters. She didn't get angry when our fingers were stained with black ink. She would sit on a chair in the book room, reading her books, as we wrote the words dozens of times, trying to achieve the penmanship my mother wanted, which was no easy task.

"This letter is tilting to the right, and this one to the left. The letters must all be moving in the same direction, and they must be beautiful and consistent. Repeat these three more times."

She said it in such a firm way that it was no use telling her that we were hungry or tired. In quiet moments, she would tell us about the city and about her father, our grandfather, who copied out books, and also sold them. She told us how his fame as an excellent scribe reached far and wide, and that people came from great distances to get him to copy their books and write their messages in his beautiful script.

Twice a week, she would give us lessons in the herbal arts. She told us about different kinds of herbs, where each was found, and what they were used for. We spent hours in the kitchen, learning to tell herbs apart by their shapes and smells, learning to mix them, and trying to pronounce their difficult names.

My father had the task of teaching us about the rest of the plants—their names, shapes, and growing seasons. He taught us the right time to prune a tree, the names of flowers, the way to distinguish different species of birds, and how to make traps for the birds—which, in spite of our protests, he would release soon after they were caught. We learned how to milk the sheep, and, on our sixth birthday, he gave us each a bow and a quiver of arrows he'd made by hand. He spent hours with us, teaching us how to pull back the string and fire our arrows.

We went with him on hunting trips up the mountain, and he would often lead us to a favorite place, a rock where you could stand and look out at the valley. He said he used to play with his friends there, and that was where they'd set traps for rabbits. We wanted him to tell us about this mysterious village, the place we lived alongside but didn't know. He told us stories from his childhood, and about the first time he visited the city, and about the story of the curse.

Once, after my father returned from a trip to the city, where he'd been for several days, he disappeared for a full day. He returned to us at night, tousle-headed and exhausted. He started to leave again the next morning, and we tried to catch up with him to find out where he was going. When he ordered us to go home, we were very upset. My mother was the only one who knew where he was off to, and every morning he'd take along a basket of food, which she'd hand him with a smile. In the evening, we could hear them whisper.

After two months of these frequent disappearances, my father came back one evening and told my mother, "I finished!"

My mother smiled. "Your dream's come true! Tonight, we'll celebrate with a fancy supper."

I asked him, "What's your dream that came true? Is it the reason you've been disappearing?"

He picked me up and spun me around the room.

"I built a bridge over the valley, and now people from the village can go to the city whenever they want! Isn't that wonderful? Maybe I'll take you there this spring."

"I've missed the city so much," Mama said to me and Shams. "I'll show you our house there, and I'll take you to all the places I used to go when I was small. You'll meet my relatives, and I'll buy you beautiful dresses and shoes embroidered with gold!"

My mother was so filled with emotion that she started to cry.

"Don't worry," my father told us. "Those are tears of joy."

That night, when I went to sleep, I dreamt of the city, with its buildings, markets, streets, and people.

We woke the next morning to the sound of Aisha screaming and wailing. We all ran outside, where Aisha was slapping a hand against her head.

"Look! Look!"

Gray smoke rose up out of the valley and into the mountain, forming a black cloud over the trees.

"Wait here," my father said.

Then he disappeared from view behind the mountain. It wasn't long before he returned, shaking his head.

"They burned the bridge," he said, his voice cracking.

He didn't say anything else, but went and closed himself up in the book room.

My father stayed locked up in the book room for a full week, and no one was allowed in except for my mother, who brought in plates of food. She usually brought them back full, without a single bite missing. Mama would be in there only a few minutes, whispering with my father. Then she'd come out with an anxious expression. To our eager looks, she would reply, "He'll come out soon."

Sadness hung over the house, and we missed Baba's playfulness and his voice. We spoke in whispers, as if we didn't want to disturb his solitude, without knowing exactly what had happened. Even Aisha, who used to sing in her powerful voice, stopped her songs and spoke in a whisper. Whenever we asked her about my father, she'd say, "God will restore him health and strength."

On the evening of the eighth day, my father burst from the book room, carrying a paper covered in shapes and lines. In a loud voice, he said, "I'll build the bridge again." He lifted up Shams and me, and he started singing and spinning around the room like a man possessed.

At the sound of my father's voice, my mother came out of the kitchen, smiling as she wiped away her tears.

"You'll build it again, and I'll help you. We'll all help you."

Suddenly we heard a soft rapping at the door, and my father lowered us from his shoulders and gave my mother a puzzled look. She just shrugged her shoulders in surprise as my father went to the door.

We heard him greeting his guest.

"Welcome, welcome, my dear friend Omar. Come in."

Omar was a little older than my father, short and very thin, with a long beard that had begun to go gray.

"Excuse me for coming at such a late hour," Omar said in his deep voice. "But you know the people of this village are not forgiving. And if they knew…"

"Please," my father said. "Sit down."

Shams and I approached the stranger who sat before us, surveying and studying him. This was the first time we'd seen one of the village men up close. Curiosity pushed us forward, just as fear tugged us back, trapping us in the sitting-room doorway.

My father saw us hanging there and told us, "Come on, don't be scared, this is my old friend, Omar." Then he pointed to us, proudly. "These are my daughters, Shams and Qamar."

"God is Great" the man said, smiling. "This is a beauty among beauties," he said, nodding at Shams. "While this is a wonder among all of God's wonders."

My mother entered the room, and the stranger stood up and looked at the floor.

"Please," she said to him. "Sit."

He sat hesitantly, still looking at the ground. Then he spluttered, directing his words at my father.

"I'm truly sorry that the villagers burned the bridge, and I've come to tell you that some friends and I welcomed the idea, even if we didn't dare show it. But the Village Elders said the bridge would lead to depravity—if the men could go down to the city at any time of year, they could return with more curses, since Suleiman's leaving caused a curse, and, I'm sorry…"

He looked back down at the floor.

"And me, too," my father said. "But there was no new curse. And we—my wife and I—think the curse wasn't because of Suleiman's leaving. Perhaps there are other reasons, and we believe it's time that—"

"What do you mean, Saeed?" Omar interrupted. "Don't start with this heresy."

"It isn't heresy," my father said with a smile. "And you, Omar…If you weren't afraid of the Village Elders, you'd go to the city and never come back. Don't tell me otherwise."

Omar stood suddenly, as if bitten by a snake.

"I don't want to talk about this. I just came to tell you how sorry I was that the bridge was burned. God be with you."

And he left, making a simple bow to my mother, while still looking at the floor.

My father closed the door behind him and came back, rubbing his hands together.

"There is no power nor strength except in God!"

"Alright," my mother said. "And then?"

"I'll start rebuilding the bridge tomorrow," he said, resolved.

I was sitting in an olive tree, and Shams was begging me to help her climb up, when I saw two black shadows among the trees. I was terrified, and I almost fell right out of the tree onto my sister, who was still calling to me, pleading. I didn't hesitate for a moment, but dropped to the ground and grabbed my sister's hand, running to my mother and pulling my sister behind me.

"Mama, Mama!" I called. "Ghosts…ghosts!"

My mother came out, drying her hands on a bit of cloth, and stood in front of the door. I raced up, and Shams tried to hide behind my mother's back as we looked out from behind her.

There were two women from the village, dressed in black robes, like the woman who had visited us a month before. They covered their faces with the edges of their cloaks. The two women stood in front of the house and stared at my mother for a long moment, as though they wanted to be sure no powerful forces would appear around her. Then they looked at us, and one of them addressed us.

"By God's glory and grace!"

The women stood there, staring at us until my mother spoke.

"Come in."

The two women followed my mother into the book room, and she closed the door behind them. When we tried to protest, Aisha seized our wrists with her strong hands and dragged us behind her into the kitchen.

My mother stayed in the book room with the two women for a long time. Then we heard the door to the room open, the sound of feet, and the sound of the front door being closed.

When my mother walked into the kitchen, she had a triumphant smile on her face, like the one she wore when she'd succeeded in making a new salve, or when she'd discovered a new type of herb.

She didn't say anything. She just shared a meaningful look with Aisha. Then she instructed us, "Go and get a few tomatoes from the garden."

When we tried to protest, she gave us a firm look.

"Now."

When my father came back in the evening, Shams and I greeted him with news of the two women who had come to see my mother. My father gave my mother a curious look, and she smiled. "Let your father wash up first, so we can have supper."

At supper, she said to my father, "Your strange witch wife helped two women from the village today." Then she laughed, "You won't believe the stories they tell about me in the village."

"I believe it." My father smiled. "This is my village, and I know it only too well."

3

DEPARTURE

How long it's been! And how far off it seems, as though it were another lifetime. I would never have guessed that I'd leave the village forever, with only one book. I didn't even know that I would leave, much less that my journey would continue for this many years. Yet I can remember the details from those days so vividly—I can still conjure up the smell of the herbs my mother would mix and scald and boil. I can still remember the scent of Aisha's sweat as she put me in her lap and combed my hair. It was a time of great events—events that would change the village forever.

My mother was obsessed with the tree, about which the village's founder had once dreamt, and she asked for some of its leaves and a piece of its bark. Then she disappeared into the book room for two days.

After that, she shifted to the kitchen, moving between the two rooms in a state of intense concentration, without talking to anyone. If not for Aisha, the house would have been an impossible mess.

One day, she asked my father to bring her a pair of rabbits from the city, one male and one female. Another time, she asked us girls to gather up frogs. The villagers had been forced to buy female animals because of the curse that hung over the village, although they refused to allow in female humans for the same reason—marriage, that is.

There came a day when my mother went into the book room and closed herself in, not coming out until evening. When she emerged, her eyes were swollen and her face was pale. Her hair was mussed and her clothes disheveled. In a hoarse voice, she said, "Call your father."

My father came in a hurry, and my mother ran to him and hugged him tightly, exclaiming, "I've figured it out…I've figured out the curse! Ha-haha!" And suddenly she broke away from my father and danced and spun around by herself, laughing.

Had my mother lost her mind? The long hours she'd spent inside the book room must have led her to madness. We'd never seen her in such a state before. My father took her hands and tried to get her to sit and be calm.

"Quickly, bring her a cup of water," he said to Aisha.

My mother stood.

"I don't want water. I want to dance and shout and sing!"

She danced a few turns around the room.

"There's no curse," she said, gasping. "There's no magic. It's all superstition!"

We were still in shock when she repeated it.

"It's that big cursed *tree* that's the reason."

She could scarcely catch her breath, and it wasn't until she was tired of dancing and spinning that she sat down and took my father's hand.

"Your sacred tree, Saeed! That tree secretes a substance that causes the sex of the fetus to be only male—men, donkeys, sheep, cows, horses, even insects, ha!"

My father noticed we were still standing there in shock, amazement etched on our faces, and he motioned for us to sit down.

"Can you please explain this calmly and without all this

emotion, Jawaher? Because I don't understand any of it."

My mother took deep breaths until she got her emotions under control.

"The great sacred tree, the one that men sit around in the evenings, the cursed tree that women are not allowed to come near, lest its leaves fall."

"I know…and?"

"The big tree that's there, at the edge of the village, and nobody knows its name or species."

My father was losing patience.

"And…Jawaher?"

"I found a substance in its leaves that affects the sex of the fetus…Wait here."

She disappeared into the book room and returned with two books, opening the first.

"Look, isn't this your tree?"

She opened the second book.

"And it's here, too." She handed him the two books. "Read what's written here," she said, pointing to the pages.

My father looked up from the books.

"But these are from one of the islands off the coast of China!"

"Keep reading," said my mother.

"It's sacred there, and its leaves are used in natural medicines, and celebrations are held around it every year, because of…"

My mother looked at him.

"Finish it, finish…It's because of the tree's ability to affect the fetus. That's why women go to the island, presenting gifts and making vows. In the hopes of giving birth to a boy.

"But," my father said, as he closed the book, "how did it get *here*?"

"That is one of God's wonders!"

"But this tree has been here hundreds of years," he said. "Why now?"

"Read here," my mother said, pointing to another page. "The tree takes a long time—up to two hundred years—to reach full maturity."

"Alright," he said. "We know the secret. But that doesn't mean we've found the solution."

"Ahhh," she said, as though my father had thrown cold water on her, and she sat heavily on the floor. "That's the hardest part. You'll have to convince the men not to go near that tree, because I'm sure of this, from my experiments with the male and female animals you brought from the city. I'm sure this tree is the cause."

This was one of two important events in the village.

The other was no less of a shock than the discovery of the curse. After the death of the village headman, my father's friend Omar was chosen to lead the Elders' Council. My father was overjoyed at this news, which he thought meant his isolation would be over, that the silence would be broken.

I was fifteen when these things happened, and I still hadn't seen the village, nor did I even know its outlines.

Soon after these events, great changes started to come over my mother. She grew increasingly pale, and she lost weight so quickly she could hardly stay on her feet. Our worry increased when she began to cough. At first, the coughing fits were spread out, followed by a rattling sound and shortness of breath. The coughing fits grew closer together. When one ended, my mother would be so exhausted she could scarcely catch her breath. Then spots of blood appeared on her handkerchief.

My father and Aisha tried everything, but none of their treatments succeeded—herbs, remedies, medicines my father brought from the city. My mother was steadily growing worse. It was hard for me to see her so weak, as she'd always been strong, always moving. She always had an answer for any question and knew just what to do. She was strict, but very tender. And now she was nearly a ghost, lying in bed, needing help to change her position on the pillow.

That spring, my mother died. She left behind an emptiness that no one and nothing could fill. Shams and I spent hours sitting in her room, or in the book room, weeping over our loss. Aisha moved from one room to the next not knowing what to do, as if she were looking everywhere for my mother. But it was my poor father who couldn't be parted from her, and he made a grave for her between the olive trees beside our house. He would sit there all day, crying and talking to her. "Why did you leave me, Jawaher? Why did you leave me?"

At night, he would sleep beside her grave. Despite our pleas, he refused food and wouldn't go into the house, even to wash. He was unmoved by hours of tears or pleas that he come inside and eat something. Even his friend Omar, who visited several times, failed to convince him. We felt helpless in the face of his insistence on joining our mother in death. It was as if he were rushing through the days in order to meet her again, and he grew weak and withered.

It seemed he'd been struck by madness—his tears would change to sudden laughter, and then he would go back to crying. My father stayed like this for a month. As he grew ever weaker, we grew ever more helpless and defeated.

Then, one sunny morning, Aisha found my father dead, his hand on my mother's grave. We made him a grave beside hers, and thus we two were orphaned, and we had no one in this world.

A week after my father's death, I was in the book room reading, trying to forget my sorrows, when I heard voices outside the house. When I came outside, I found a group of women gathered there, weeping. One of the women stepped forward, carrying something in her arms. When she came nearer, she lowered a newborn baby calf to the ground.

"It's a she!" she said through her tears.

The woman went on.

"It's thanks to your mother, who we wronged by saying she was a witch. Your mother is a saint!"

Oh, how I wished my mother were alive to see this victory with her own eyes, and to share the women's joy at the end of the curse. The woman who carried the infant cow went with the others to my mother's grave. She set down the female calf beside my mother's grave and loudly recited a passage from the Quran, with the other women joining in. Then one of them took out an oil lamp, lit it, and set it atop my mother's grave before they all left together.

With the birth of the first female in the long-cursed village, my mother was transformed from a strange witch into a saint. From then on, whenever a female of any species was born, the women of the village came to her grave and laid on it either a lamp, or flowers, or the branch of a tree. My mother's grave became a shrine. We grew used to seeing women arrive to sit beside the grave, recite from the Quran, and leave something behind.

Three months passed in this state of intense sorrow; all of us only dressed in black. And then came a day when Aisha, who seemed to have suddenly aged and gone gray, spoke.

"Your mother told me that, if ever something happened to her or your father, I should take you two to her brother's house in the city. So, it's time to leave."

Shams was excited by this idea and began to pack up her clothes and things, as the notion of living in the city set her alight with enthusiasm. But I refused to leave the house, and the memories of my childhood, and of my mother and father. The more Shams prepared herself to leave, the more tightly I clung to my memories.

Shams tried to convince me that there was nothing and no one left for us in this ungrateful village. She tried to tempt me with the pleasures of the city, while Aisha tried to convince me to carry out my mother's wishes. She said she was afraid to leave me alone among the wolves.

The day of their departure came, and Shams wept and clung to me, saying through her tears that she wouldn't leave without me, and she began to unpack her dresses from their boxes and to throw them on the ground. She refused to calm down until I promised I would join them soon. Shams kept waving as she walked away, until she disappeared among the trees. For a moment, I thought of catching up and asking her to wait for me. But then I looked to the house behind me, and to my parents' graves, and I went back inside alone.

After Shams' departure three years went by. I no longer remember the details, as the monotonous days ran from one to the next, indistinguishable. In these three years, I did nothing but read. Sometimes, from my window, I would see women moving around my mother's grave, before they left something and walked away in silence.

Days and nights passed with me absorbed in reading. Then, when there were no more books to read, I knew it was time to leave.

The headman Omar came to bid me farewell. I told him I would leave the house as it was, just as my parents had left it. I would take nothing but a few items of clothing. I'd leave the books to the villagers, for one day they would lift the ban on reading. I would take only one book on my journey. I gathered my things into a small bag, put *Wondrous Journeys* among them, and closed the door. I said farewell to my parents and walked toward the bridge, without looking back even once.

Shams greeted me with shouts of joy. She had married a trader from our mother's large family and given birth to twins, a boy and a girl. I found her as happy as if she'd been born to become a wife and mother. She said her husband was a good man, that he respected and loved her, and gave her everything she asked. She said that Aisha had died two years before.

Upon hearing of Aisha's death, I felt that I had become orphaned again. I could not imagine life without her. She had always been there, a natural part of life's scenes, like my mother's smile, my father's love, and the olive trees outside the house. With Aisha's death, a big, empty hole opened in my heart, a void impossible to fill.

May your soul find peace, Aisha. I will always miss you.

For nearly six months, I stayed with Shams. I loved her two children, and I spent most of my time playing with them and telling them stories. My sister's husband encouraged me to consider marriage, but I wouldn't think of it. There was only one idea that seized my thoughts and my spirit—travel. I wanted to fulfill my mother's wish to travel to all the wondrous countries she and my father had talked about in the book I had brought with me. I wanted to know other countries and other people.

There came a day when my sister's husband grew joyously happy and said that he had great news for me. "The prince of this city has asked for your hand in marriage. He heard about your beauty, intelligence, and wide knowledge, and he wants to have you as his wife!"

That was my sign to leave, since I didn't want to marry, and I didn't want to make my sister's husband the object of the prince's anger—this prince who already had four wives. My sister's husband said the prince would divorce one of them to marry me—this man who already had enough women in his harem for every day of the year. Shams and her husband tried to convince me to stay, and the two babies cried. Yet I was decided.

"But where will you go?" Shams asked. "An unmarried girl, heading out alone. This is madness!"

I told her I would travel to Jerusalem, and then I would do as God willed.

Shams' husband found me a place in a caravan that was heading south to Jerusalem among some traders he knew, consigning me to their goodness. As I climbed up onto the camel, Shams and the children were crying. Their tears did not stop as I set off into the unknown.

2

4
THE JOURNEY

On the first day, the road through the plains was flat, and we traveled quickly, as we sat on our rhythmically swaying camels. Before sunset, the caravan stopped at an inn set on a high, winding road, and I was happy to climb down to the ground after a long day of being carried on a camel's back.

In the section of the inn reserved for women, I threw myself down on my bed, wondering if it really was possible for me to continue this journey, or if I should go back to Shams and her two children in the city. Then a woman approached me and asked, "Are you traveling alone?"

Her affectionate tone reminded me of my mother's. I nodded, and she sat beside me on the bed, gazing into my face.

"You don't have any relatives in the caravan?"

I told her I didn't.

Surprised, she asked, "And how is it your family allows you to travel alone?"

I told her I was visiting some relatives in Jerusalem—which was a lie! She asked me about them and where they lived, and I paused in confusion.

Then I remembered the name of a Jerusalem family I'd read about in one of the books I'd left behind in the village. I told her the name and said they lived near the site of the Noble Sanctuary.

She nodded. "An excellent family."

She said we were the only two women in the caravan, although I hadn't noticed her before. She was traveling with her husband and son, who worked as a clerk for the city's judge. Then she got up and opened one of her leather bags. She drew out a box of sweets and offered them to me. Grateful, I took a little, even though I was afraid that she'd ask more questions I wouldn't be able to answer about my alleged family in Jerusalem, and I'd be forced to continue lying.

"Maybe we should sleep," I said, "since the caravan will leave at dawn."

The next morning, we continued on our way as the sun began its shy rise from behind the mountains, and the sky rapidly changed from black to blue to greenish, and then to orange. When I was in our village, I'd watched the sun rise every day. Yet this dawn, the sight was amazing. In this magic moment, I felt myself floating through the air, the scent of the autumn morning enlivening my senses. There was a faint sound of someone singing that came from the back of the caravan, which intensified the magic. But then, when the sun rose and turned up its heat, my doubts and fears about the trip returned.

The woman's voice broke into my anxieties.

"These relatives of yours, are they on your father's side or your mother's?"

I lied again.

"They're my maternal uncles."

The woman went silent, as if this new information I'd provided had convinced her, and she told me about her son, who worked as a scribe in the city, and how he'd gotten such fine work on account of his intelligence, wit, and broad scientific knowledge. After that, she went on to talk about her grandchildren. I thought of Shams and her two children, and my throat tightened.

By the time we arrived at the inn the following night, I knew the woman's life story, how she'd come to be married, and how many sons and daughters she had. I knew what her sons did for a living, how she'd married off her three daughters, and the names of their husbands. She described their homes in minute detail, especially that of the middle one, who lived in a real palace. The third day, she seemed to be waiting for me to take my turn and speak, for me to tell the story of my life, as she had. When I remained silent for a long time, she started me off.

"I've told you everything about me. Won't you tell me something about yourself?"

I had to say something. But would this lady believe the story of my village and its curse, and of my mother, the strange witch who became a saint? So, I decided to imagine a story, and I began with, "My parents had seven boys and six girls…"

"It was the custom to send the seventh girl in each family to serve the prince," I said. "When a girl moves in, she becomes the property of the prince, remaining in his service, and at his command, until her death. She's allowed neither to marry nor to leave the palace.

"When my mother gave birth to me, and discovered I was a girl, she started screaming and pleading, such that my father tried to hide my birth from public knowledge, telling everyone he had a son. My mother dressed me in boys' clothes and cut my hair short, but as I grew, it became difficult to hide my womanly traits. My father was one of the most important merchants in the city, and he had a partner he considered a friend, who he entrusted with his secrets. But this man was spiteful because he had never been able to have any children. Because of his jealousy toward my father, he told the prince about me. The prince sent soldiers to our house, and they told my father he had one week to get me ready to go to the palace. My father could do nothing to protect me and asked my mother to prepare me for my fate. My mother wept and shouted, 'Better that she be born dead than that my heart be scorched by this separation!'

"But then I came up with an idea. On the last night before I was to go to the palace, I opened the door to the well inside our courtyard. There, I left my robe and slippers before I fled to my aunt's house. In the morning, when my family saw the slippers and robe, everyone thought I had thrown myself into the well, and my family believed there had been a great tragedy. I hid at my aunt's for two months before my aunt's husband found this caravan headed for Jerusalem, which I joined. And here we are."

When I finished relating my story, the woman was weeping, and she stretched out her arm as though she wanted to take my hand in hers. "You have suffered so much! Consider me like a mother to you, my daughter."

We spent the rest of the day in silence.

The next day, at sunset, we reached the outskirts of Jerusalem. The hazy mist of the afternoon made the golden rays of the setting sun appear to be dancing with the red twilight. It was a majestic sight that made a person feel their smallness, and the golden Dome of the Rock shone like a beacon guiding ships to safety, guiding souls to find peace. My face was wet with happy tears, and I gazed on this dazzling light with fear, faith, and love.

My traveling companion saw my astonishment.

"It's amazing, is it not?"

I nodded, not trusting myself to speak.

"And now, my daughter, tell me, with God as your witness, do you really have relatives in Jerusalem?"

"Of course," I said. But then I shook my head. "The truth is I don't know anyone in this city."

"Then you will be a beloved guest and daughter to me, and you will stay with me as long as God wills it."

I tried to reject her generous invitation, while at the same time I was afraid she would withdraw it in the face of my determination.

"I can't possibly allow you to sleep in an inn with strangers!" she said. "I won't accept a refusal."

And so Um Najmuddin kept her promise to host me in her home, where I was to be nurtured and cared for as her own child, as though I filled a void left by the absence of sons and daughters left at home.

Her husband, Abu Najmuddin, treated me like a loving father would treat his daughter. Every day, before he went to the market, he'd ask if I needed anything.

I spent three months in this peace and quiet, and I grew used to a restful life with Um Najmuddin. Some days, we wandered the market, and she was the best guide to the city of Jerusalem, in which she'd been born and raised. We visited the Church of the Holy Sepulchre, and I lit a candle for my parents' souls. We visited the Mosque of al-Aqsa and the Noble Sanctuary, and I was amazed by the inventiveness of the decorative motifs, and that there were so many different people out in the courtyards. But the best part of these trips was to walk in the market, between shops crammed with people. In the Herb Market, the smells of the different spices mixed with the scent of fresh fruit and vegetables sold by village women.

The other thing I greatly enjoyed was sitting at the *mashrabiya*, a window bay where there was a wide area to sit that was covered with a soft mattress. The window itself was screened with beautiful, intricately carved wooden latticework that hid the sitter, so I could see the street without being seen. I loved observing people, the way they walked, their habits, the way they gestured when they talked.

Then one cold winter day, Um Najmuddin was ill in bed. As I cared for her and tried to help her, it brought back memories of my mother's illness. I grew anxious and afraid I might lose this mother just as I'd lost my own. Abu Najmuddin brought the doctor, who prescribed several medicines and ointments, but she didn't get better. In fact, her condition worsened. When the doctor returned, I suggested some of the herbs my mother had used in similar cases. The doctor gave me a patronizing look.

"Is this young lady a doctor?" he asked sarcastically.

"No," I said.

"And is this young lady an expert in the science of herbal medicines?"

Before I could answer, he reprimanded me sharply.

"Please do not interfere in things you cannot understand. Leave these things to those with specialist knowledge."

Then he wrote her prescriptions for more medicine.

When the doctor left, Abu Najmuddin asked me how I knew about these herbs, and if they really would be useful for his wife's condition. I told him that my mother had used them in the village.

"The village? But you told us you were from the city," he said in surprise.

"Yes, my mother's from the village, but I was born and lived in the city."

He didn't seem convinced.

"And how did your mother know about herbal medicines?"

"She read a lot of medical books and learned a few things from them."

Abu Najmuddin stood in silence, staring into my face as though he'd discovered something new.

"Give me the list of herbs. If they don't work, at least they won't harm her."

Later, he returned, carrying the herbs I'd requested. I mixed them carefully, adding the amounts I still remembered, boiled them, and had Um Najmuddin drink the concoction before I left her to sleep.

Abu Najmuddin said to me, "Come here, my daughter. I want to talk with you."

He sat on the cushioned window seat that overlooked the street and motioned for me to sit beside him.

"You have become like a daughter to us in this house, and my wife and I have both loved and respected you. In these past months, you've been a good companion to my wife in her loneliness. But I think you're hiding something from me, and I don't believe the story of the seventh girl that you told my wife. So, is there anything you want to tell me? Consider me like your father, and don't be scared."

I looked into this man's face and saw that he meant his loving kindness. Abu Najmuddin had welcomed me into his home without knowing much about me, and he truly had treated me like a daughter. I felt ashamed that I hadn't told them the truth, as though I'd stolen affection and love from him and his wife.

"I was afraid that if I told you my story, you wouldn't believe me."

"Tell me, daughter," he said. "And don't be afraid."

And so I began my story from the moment I was born in a tent at the foot of a mountain, and told of our isolation and the curse, and how my mother was able to solve the village mystery and lift the curse, the death of my parents, living with my sister, and how I really had escaped being wed to a prince.

This good man listened to all of it in silence. After I had finished, he remained silent, looking at the many-colored carpet beneath his feet. So, I too looked at the rug and waited for his reaction.

"That is one strange story!"

Then we sat in silence for what felt like an eon before he continued.

"This is your home, and you can stay here as our beloved daughter."

And he didn't say anything else.

The next day brought a marked improvement in the health of Um Najmuddin. She slept through the night pain-free, and she woke up cheerful, asking for food. Abu Najmuddin's joy was beyond description, and when he came back that evening, he was carrying a package of books and handed them to me.

"You must have missed reading," he said.

Winter passed, cold and monotonous, and I spent most of my time sitting at the window and reading, as well as sharing conversations with Um Najmuddin, who had recovered completely. And thus I stayed in this dignified home with these lovely people. But by spring, I began to feel an insistent urge to leave and continue on my travels. Abu Najmuddin noticed my distress.

"Are you ill, my daughter?" he asked.

I told him I wasn't.

"Is there something bothering you? Has someone caused you harm?"

I told him I was happy and comfortable with them, but that the urge to travel was prickling inside me.

Abu Najmuddin thought for a while.

"If you mean to travel, then I won't stop you. But where will you go, my daughter?"

"I've heard of a scholar in Morocco who is said to be a

marvel of knowledge and wisdom, and I want to travel there to learn at his side."

"But the road is long and dangerous for a girl alone!"

"God protects those who believe."

"But where is the final destination, my daughter?"

"As I walk, all paths open before me."

And so it was that, at the beginning of spring, I decided to leave with a caravan headed to Gaza, and from there to Egypt. Abu and Um Najmuddin wept, and Um Najmuddin clung to me, asking me to stay a few more months.

Abu Najmuddin pulled her back, saying, "Let her go in God's hands." Then he turned to me.

"My daughter, this is your house and we are your family, and if one day you return, you'll find this house open to you. If you need anything at any time, I'll be there for you."

Then he gave me a bag filled with silver coins.

And I headed to another caravan.

There's not much I remember of the journey from Jerusalem to Gaza, and it passed with so little trouble that by now I've almost forgotten that I even made the trip. Except for one thing I can't forget—the sea! It was the first time in my life that I saw this vast stretch of blue. It was the first time I smelled the salt, heard the sound of the waves, and saw the white foam clinging to the beach before the wave draws it away, only to throw it back again.

I felt my heart cease beating, and my breaths nearly stop. It was as though the amazing sea were inviting me to join it and stay there in its embrace. I did not know then that I would share many stories with the sea.

Abu Najmuddin had given me a letter to carry to a friend of his in Gaza, and this man was as good to me as Abu Najmuddin had been. He refused to let me stay in the khan and opened his house to me, inviting me to stay with his family. He had four daughters who were much younger than me. In Gaza, I discovered three things I'll never forget: the sea, the family of Abu Hassan, and the taste of fish.

I didn't stay in Gaza for long. I wanted to continue my journey before the dreadful heat of summer was upon us, so I asked Abu Hassan to find me a caravan bound for Egypt. I said my farewells to the family and seated myself on the camel, which I was now accustomed to riding for long stretches. Then, I headed off toward Egypt.

The caravan to Egypt was much larger than my two previous caravans. This one was loaded down with soap from Nablus, salt from the Dead Sea, olives from the mountains of Jerusalem, and oranges from Gaza. The caravan would return after a month, with cotton and pilgrims headed to Jerusalem. As we crossed the desert, the weather was very hot by day and the evenings were very cold. At night, we would crowd around the fire and try to warm our bodies. People sat around this flickering fire singing, remembering other trips, and telling stories and tall tales. Formalities quickly slipped away, and out flowed jokes, tales, and songs. We traveled as a family to the end of the journey, connected by a shared fate and a strong bond.

On one of these cold nights, after we'd finished eating and the cups of bitter coffee began to circulate, one of the women asked if anyone could tell a story. I said I knew some tales. But then my cheeks reddened, and I felt I'd been too hasty and wouldn't be able to tell a tale in front of such a large group. But I couldn't turn back, not when I was surrounded by all these expectant looks, waiting for me to stave off the cold of the night with my story. So I told them a story I'd read in a book, about a sailor lost in the Sea of Darkness, who remained there for many years, fighting the waves, horrors, and monsters of the sea, until finally he triumphed and returned to his family.

After I'd finished this tale, the people around me were quiet, as though a spell had been laid on them. From then on, they asked me to tell them a new story every night, and they would hover around me, eagerly waiting for me to begin.

On one of those nights, when I was telling them a tale: "... and so the brave knight took up the sword that had fallen, and blood was streaming from his arm. He approached the ghoul, who said to him in a terrifying voice—"

"Stay where you are and don't move!"

People cried out in terror, and my tongue froze in astonishment—this was not my voice and it was not part of the story! Our caravan had been surrounded by a large group of highwayman, their faces concealed by black scarves, and their swords and daggers raised.

"Resist, and we'll kill you all," one of them shouted to the men of the caravan.

Women covered their mouths with their hands so they wouldn't scream while the men sat on the ground, shamefaced, unable to confront this brutal-looking army of bandits, and careful not to do anything that would get someone killed. When day broke, we were still sitting on the sand. The thieves had ordered the women to keep feeding the fire all night, as they told the men to stay seated with their hands tied behind their backs.

The next day, the gang ordered us to keep going. So the caravan walked on in silence, and anyone who slowed us down was struck by a lash. At night, when everyone was sitting around the fire, we ate, with most of the food going to the highwaymen.

"Which of you was telling the story last night?" their leader suddenly demanded.

No one spoke, but all eyes turned toward me, and I began to tremble and pulled my cloak tight around my body.

"Come now, and we'll hear the rest of the story," the man said.

I stood on feet quivering with fear. I pulled the mantle of my cloak over my head and held a bit of cloth over my face, exactly as the women of my village had once done. He gestured that I should sit beside him, and his smell was overpowering—sweat, tobacco, and the musk of a body that had not known soap and water for years.

"Go on," the man insisted.

His yellowed teeth beneath his mustache were like the teeth of a wolf about to seize its prey. I was shaking badly, and I had no idea how to tell a tale in such a frightening situation. How I wish I had not opened my mouth on that night!

"Come on!" the man shouted.

I began to speak, my words faltering, my voice barely emerging from my throat. The man slapped me across the face.

"I don't like to be kept waiting. I said *go on*!"

As I went on with the story, the blood from my lips mixed with my salty tears. When I finished, the head of the gang shouted at me in a voice that made my bones tremble.

"I don't want it to end like that! I don't like virtuous knights! Make the ghoul win. Come on…do the ending again!"

"But…" I said.

"What?" he shouted, rising from his place.

I was afraid he was going to hit me again, and I drew back, finishing the story and making the evil ghoul victorious over the brave knight.

The thief applauded.

"Ahh, I do like happy endings."

And so, the leader of the highwaymen called on me every night to tell him a story. And every night, he meddled in the details and made the story take the path he wanted. But then, one day, he came up to me.

"You'll fetch me a good price on the slave market," he said.

5

PRINCESS NOOR AL-HUDA

I'm not sure how long we walked in that hot desert. The highwaymen were quick to anger, and they wouldn't hesitate to strike anyone who slowed down. Our hands were tied with rope, each of us bound to the next in a long chain, so that walking was very difficult and slow. I stumbled over another traveler, losing my footing, and when I pulled myself back up, I felt the bite of the lash against my back. It sent me tumbling to the ground, along with all the men and women to whom I was tied. This provoked the head of the gang, who shouted at me in a terrifying voice, "If I didn't think you'd bring me a good price, I'd kill you now!"

I blamed myself for insisting on joining a caravan that went through the desert instead along the sea. I'd stupidly thought the desert was magic, as it was in the songs of poets, and I'd wanted to experience that magic. I couldn't understand why they wouldn't allow us to ride on the camels—we'd go a lot faster. But I didn't dare ask this out loud.

Finally, when I thought I was about to die, the man in front of me whispered, "Look, we're near Cairo!" I was exhausted from walking and needed to rest. At that moment, my fiercest wish was for a drink of cold water.

This whole time, I hadn't allowed myself to think about what might be coming, or about what would happen if they sold me in the slave market. It had taken all my physical and mental energies just to put one foot in front of the other without collapsing from exhaustion. If only we hadn't been captured by these men, I would have entered Cairo admiring the streets, the people, the buildings, the parks! But I entered it without my freedom, and I wanted this journey to end. I no longer cared about my fate or where I'd end up. I wanted only to stop walking and get some rest.

The number in our caravan had been reduced by more than half by the time we reached Cairo. Some of the older people had died of thirst, and the gang had only selected boys younger than fifteen and most women—especially young women—to continue with them on their journey. The rest of the older men and women had been left in the sizzling desert without a single drop of water.

We walked in a single line through Cairo's wide streets, our hands still tied behind our backs, the highwaymen driving us to market as they would a herd of cattle. Some people stopped in the road to look at us, and one of them murmured, "*La hawla wa la quwwata 'illa bi Allah.* There is no strength nor power except in God."

At last we arrived at a house in one of the narrow back alleys, and we had to duck so we could pass through the small door. We found ourselves in a large courtyard that had a withered tree at its center. An old woman emerged from one of the green doors that surrounded the courtyard, and the head of the gang said to her, "Feed them, and don't dare take off their restraints! And this is for you." He threw her a bag of gold dinars, which the old woman held against her ear, shaking it so she could hear the coins inside.

That night, I couldn't sleep for fear of what was to come. *A slave? How could a free woman become a slave, just like that? One moment I am traveling to what I thought would be a new future, the next I am a slave? Who would buy me? What would my life be like?* I cursed the day I had decided to travel with this caravan. When the sun rose, I had not yet shut my eyes, which were swollen from weeping. The old woman came to us, and our restraints were removed, one at a time, so that we could wash ourselves with water from a barrel that was no cleaner than our faces.

The thieves stepped into the courtyard where we were gathered. They'd brought some slave traders with them, and they ordered us to stand. The traders examined us in minute detail, opening our mouths to be sure our teeth were in good condition, asking some of the women to show their breasts, turning us around and tugging at our hair, asking us to bend over and turn our backs and squat and stand before they went off to a far corner of the courtyard to negotiate a price.

An argument broke out between a slaver and the thieves about the price they should pay for me. They would point at me, then the slaver would raise his hand in the air and bring it down. I didn't hear what they were saying, but I understood from their gestures that the thieves wanted a higher price for me than they were asking for the other women, and the man was trying to convince them to lower it.

All of the traders took their "merchandise" and left. The one who bought me was very short and fat, breathing hard from the abundance of flesh he had accumulated. His beard was long, and he'd turned it orange with henna so that it was a different color from his eyebrows and mustache.

After paying the thieves, he pointed to me, two other women, and a child of twelve. "Follow me."

We walked out behind him into the sun and through the wide streets once again, until we reached an open yard filled with raised platforms. Every slaver stood on a platform, and behind him were the enslaved people he wanted to sell. He called out about his "goods," hoping to catch the attention of the buyers.

"This is a strong woman who can do all your housework!"

"This strong youth can run a wheat mill on less than it takes to feed a donkey!"

Our merchant began to yell about his goods between wheezing gasps. "This rare Palestinian gem can tell tales that make her fit for a Sultan or Prince! Come on, come on, who says a hundred dinars?"

"Let's see her other qualities," I heard a man say.

The slaver turned to me and ordered me to take off my clothes. But before I could utter a word in protest, I heard a woman's voice.

"Eighty dinars."

I looked to the foot of the platform to see who had shifted the slaver's attention off me, and I spotted two women dressed in rich silken robes. One of them was covering her face with a scarf of pink silk, while the second—who saved me from being shamed in front of all these people—was barefaced.

"Sayyidati," the slaver said to her, "eighty dinars is a very small price for this girl, who can beguile you with her silver tongue and delightful stories."

"Seventy dinars," the stately woman said.

"God forbid, Sayyidati, this is so little! Eighty-five."

"Eighty, and not a dinar more."

"There is no power nor strength except in God, but I've paid a great deal to get her, and I'd be losing my daily bread!"

"Eighty," she insisted.

"There is no God but God. Take her, Sayyidati, knowing I don't earn a single dirham."

The man loosened my fetters and smiled a malicious smile.

"Obey and respect your mistress."

I stepped down from the platform, and the woman indicated I should follow her and her companion. So, I did, until they were sitting in a luxurious carriage pulled by two thoroughbred Arabian horses. I wanted to climb into the carriage, but the woman motioned with her hand, "Not here, with the coachman." So, I rode beside him as he drove the horses in silence.

We crossed clean, wide, tree-lined streets and arrived at an enormous wall, overhung with jasmine trees. We approached a gate that was guarded on both sides by heavily armed men, who, upon spotting the carriage, turned to open the large gate.

Entering a tree-lined path, I could hear the birds' singing mingled with the sound of the horses' hooves striking the gravel. We drove for what seemed like a long time before the coachman stopped, and I lifted my gaze to find myself in front of a huge palace, the likes of which I'd never seen in my life. The coachman stopped by stairs that led up to the palace, and guards scrambled to open the carriage doors. As soon as the woman with the pink scarf looked up, the guards bowed before her.

The coachman whispered to me, "Your Mistress is the sister of the King. She is good, and you will be at ease in her service." He said nothing more, but nodded for me to get down from the carriage.

I stood behind the two women without knowing what to do. They were absorbed in conversation, as if they'd forgotten my presence, and then they began to walk. Finally, the one who had bought me turned and motioned for me to follow her. We climbed the stairs, and there were more guards and another door that opened to reveal an enormous hall. I gave an involuntary gasp, as the floors were covered in red carpets so thick one's foot plunged into them, and covered with images of lions fighting, while the walls were hung with portraits of kings and princes in golden frames. On the ceiling hung a chandelier lit by candles, with colors dancing on the glass like a thousand rainbows.

The woman smiled at my surprise. "Come."

We climbed a staircase in the middle of the hall, which was also covered in red carpets. On either side were wooden bannisters inlaid with gold. When we reached the first floor, the woman ordered, "Wait here." Then the two women disappeared behind one of the doors, in front of which a guard stood so motionless I took him for a statue.

I stood there, looking around. Everything suggested obscene wealth and elegant taste—I was in a king's palace! My thoughts were interrupted by the appearance of a woman dressed in simple clothes who addressed me with distaste.

"You're the new slave girl? Follow me."

When I heard the word *slave*, my heart jumped with fear. It was as though everything that had happened to me thus far hadn't been enough to make me see the truth. I followed her, saying to myself, *You're a slave now, Qamar—a slave, a slave, a slave!*

The woman disappeared behind a curtain I hadn't noticed before—it was the same color as the wall and covered with gilded decorations. Following her, I found myself walking up a long corridor covered in green carpets. Identical doors lined both walls of the corridor, and the woman opened one and stepped through it. Inside, I could see a spacious room with simple furniture and a number of beds. She gestured for me to follow, and then she opened a door at the side of the room. It was a large bathroom.

"After you've bathed, put on these clothes," she said, pointing to clothes laid out on a chair. "Then wait here. I'll find out if Her Highness will see you now."

Despite my anxious concern, I enjoyed bathing in this lovely place. The clothes they gave to me were made of a soft cotton, dyed blue and light green, and there was a long turquoise scarf. *Could I ever have imagined ending up in such a palace? And would I spend the rest of my life as a slave in a strange country?*

The thread of my thoughts was snipped when the woman entered the room without knocking.

"Her Highness will see you now."

We went back down the same corridor to stand in front of the same door where the guard still stood statue-like beside it. We stepped into a spacious and elegant room, filled with luxurious seats covered in silken cushions, and many vases of tastefully arranged yellow and orange flowers.

"Wait here," she said.

I sat down on one of the seats that stood before an engraved copper table, on which was resting a flowered vase. Suddenly, the woman returned and shouted at me.

"Stand up! Who gave you permission to sit? Go on, enter. Don't keep Her Highness waiting."

She opened a door, and I stepped into a room yet larger than the first, suffused with the smell of incense. At the head of the room was a large bed surrounded by silk curtains the color of the sky, but, before I could study the rest of the room, I heard a woman's voice.

"What's your name?"

I turned to find a mattress on the floor, covered with such an enormous number of colored silk pillows that they almost hid a woman of exquisite beauty. Beside her, on her knees, was the woman who had bought me, and then I knew she was also a slave girl.

"My name is Qamar."

I remained standing in the same place, and the second woman shouted at me, "When you meet with Her Royal Highness the Princess, you must get on your knees."

I said to myself, *I will not bow for the princess or any other,* and I lifted my head with a pride the princess didn't fail to notice.

"There's no need," the princess said. "Come sit here before me."

I sat on the thick blue carpet in front of her. She spoke in a gentle and encouraging voice that was not without an undertone of command. "And where are you from, Qamar?"

"From Palestine," I told her.

"And what has brought you to this country?"

I told her about the caravan, and the bandits who had sold me in the slave market, but she broke in, "Why did you come by caravan to Egypt?"

I told her I was on my way to Morocco.

"And what is there in Morocco?"

I thought that, if I were to tell her the truth, she wouldn't believe me. So I said, "I'm going to get some medicine for my sick mother."

"Don't you have a brother? Or a father?" she asked.

"No, I'm an orphan, Your Highness."

At that, the other slave shouted at me, "When you speak to Her Highness the Princess, say, Your *Royal* Highness."

The Princess gestured to silence her. "It's alright, Mawahib, it's alright."

Mawahib returned to her place, clearly furious.

"The trader said that you tell tales. Is that true, or have I paid eighty dinars for nothing?"

"Yes, Your Royal Highness," I said. "It's true."

"And where did you learn to tell stories?"

"From my grandmother."

"Then you will begin your storytelling this evening, and I will allow you to sleep in the *jawari* quarters."

She indicated that our interview was finished.

Mawahib rose from her place as though she wanted to

slap me, but then said, "Do you know your way to, the *jawari* quarters?"

"Yes," I told her. Then I made a simple bow to the Princess and left the room.

When I got back to the *jawari* room, I found two girls sitting side by side on a bed, whispering. As I stepped into the room, they stopped talking and looked up to study me, standing still by the door.

"You must be the new slave girl," one of them said, and I nodded.

"And why are you standing there like an idiot? Don't you speak Arabic?"

"Yes," I said in a low voice.

"What's your name?" the second one asked.

"Qamar."

"Come on in, Qamar, this bed's empty." She gestured toward the bed beside the bathroom door, and I sat on the bed feeling extremely confused.

"Where are you from, Qamar?" she asked.

"Palestine."

"I'm Yasmine and this is Kuzida."

I looked at Yasmine in confusion, not knowing how to act. Yasmine had warm brown skin, black hair falling to her waist, and clever black eyes. She wore a cotton gown like mine, except hers was red, tending toward orange. As for her friend Kuzida, well, *what sort of name was Kuzida?* She was pale-skinned, with hair verging on blonde and eyes that were tawny brown. She drew back her upper lip as she spoke, which made her look as though she were about to spit.

"And what important task did the Princess entrust to you?" Kuzida asked, looking at me with contempt.

"I'm to tell her stories," I said.

"What? They put you in the *jawari* quarters just because you *tell stories*?"

She slapped her hands together and twisted her lips with disdain, then stood, and I noticed her great height. She put on golden, brocaded slippers and disappeared into the bathroom.

"It's not you," Yasmine said. "She's always like that, but she has a kind heart. Have you eaten?"

I shook my head.

"I'll be right back," she said, and left the room.

She returned, followed by a dark-skinned slave woman who was carrying a silver tray full of dishes. Yasmine pointed to a table at the center of the room, surrounded by pillows and mattresses, and she set down the tray, then bowed and left.

"Eat," Yasmine said, gesturing to the food, and she sat down on a mattress opposite me and slowly ate an apple.

"Five girls live in this room, it is part of the *jawari* quarters, and you're the sixth. And here are the high-ranking slaves serving the princes—Mawahib, for example. She has her own room close to the Princess' suites. The higher a girl's status, the more privileges the Princess grants her. Newcomers like you usually live in a room with common slaves, in a separate quarter attached to the kitchen. Those do the hard, dirty work, like cleaning, washing, tending to the animals, and other stuff."

Then she came closer and whispered to me.

"That's why Kuzida was surprised."

I wiped my hands on a scented napkin that lay on the table. "And what do *jawari* do?" I asked. "That is…I mean…"

Yasmine smiled.

"Some work in service of the Princess Noor al-Huda. Kuzida, for instance, is responsible for choosing the Princess's clothes each morning and supervising her raiment, while I'm in charge of styling her hair."

She pointed to an empty bed in a corner of the room.

"The girl who sleeps here is responsible for arranging the Princess's quarters and choosing her flowers, Narjis and Tamayim are responsible for the Princess's food, and the rest of the girls do other things, such as overseeing the cleaning of the palace, or arranging flowers in the vases, or preparing food and presenting it to the King, and so on."

Oh, the King, I thought. *I forgot the King.*

"His Majesty is very difficult when it comes to food," Yasmine continued. "There are things he refuses to eat, like chicken and meat, and then there are things he wants to eat every day, like *molukhiya*—mallow soup!"

Then Yasmine leaned her head in closer, until her lips were almost touching my ear.

"Some people think the King is mad, and that the soothsayers who surround him have made him lose his mind. Can you imagine? The first thing he does in the morning is consult with these charlatans, and the day doesn't start until they tell him what to do, and he doesn't leave the palace unless he's with one of them. But the most dangerous among them is Jabbour. Her Highness the Princess is very afraid of him."

Then two slaves entered the room, and they looked so similar I thought they were twins. Yasmine told me these were Narjis and Tamayim, and she said, "This is Qamar, a new girl."

Both smiled pleasant smiles, and Narjis said curtly, "Welcome."

I was so relieved that Yasmine was there to help me carry out my duties and make my situation more bearable. I spent the rest of the day listening to her tales about the palace and the lives and stories of the jawari, the slave women, which was a whole new world for me. Her banter was very entertaining.

In the evening, Mawahib came and motioned for me to go with her. I followed her to the Princess' quarters, where she was sitting on a mattress with many pillows and surrounded by a large number of slave women.

"Come here, Qamar. Isn't that your name? Tell us an amusing tale."

I sat and turned to the Princess. "What would you like it to be about, ya Mawlati?"

"Tell us a story," she said. "Any story, as long as it's amusing."

I began my story with a stutter, but when I found her rapt and looking at me with her full attention, my voice gained confidence.

"…then the girl said, 'We cannot meet, for I cannot live in your world, and if I leave the world of dreams I shall die. But you can come to my world. You can leave your world and live with me.'"

Then I went silent and asked the Princess if I could have a sip of water. She gestured to one of the slave women to give me some, and when I'd taken a drink, the Princess hastened me along.

"And what happened after that? Did he leave his world?"

"The young man thought a great deal about leaving his world for that of his sweetheart," I said, "as he would be leaving his land and his family, and all that he knew, and entering a fantasy world where he too would become a dream, never to return to the real world. And so, he walked to the river and sat…"

One of the slave women handed a cluster of grapes to the Princess, but she waved them off, watching my face, waiting for me to tell the rest of the story.

"…and the face of his beloved appeared above the water, saying, 'I am waiting for you, my love,' And the young man stood quickly, looking at the image that hovered above the water, saying to it, 'You may have to wait a long time, as I have much to do here in this land.' And he left the river and went back to his own land."

When I finished my story, the Princess and all the *jawari* remained silent and motionless, until suddenly the Princess smiled and clapped her hands with pleasure, and her slave women began to applaud.

"Well done, Qamar," the Princess said, smiling. "Tomorrow, I want a story that's just as exciting." Then she gestured that I was dismissed.

And so it was that every night I would tell a new story to the Princess, who I began to discover was both kind and clever. During the days, I would wander around the palace, through its gardens and courtyards, or I would talk with Yasmine, listening to her stories about the harem and life in the palace. I began to learn more about this world. I learned that the Harem section itself was also a multilayered world. It was my good fortune to be in the section to serve the Princess and not the other section, which not only serves the King, but is also for his pleasure.

Then one day, the Princess sent me an order at an unusual time.

"I'm feeling very poorly," she said when I entered the room. "Tell me a story to lighten my mood."

I sat in my usual place, but this time there were only a few slaves in the room with the Princess. So, I told her the story of a princess who was fed up with her idle and detached life in the palace, and who wanted to live among the people as one of them. One day, she disguised herself in a maid's clothes and, dressed like this, she moved about the kingdom, where she heard many people complaining about the king. She found work in a village, as a maid for an old woman, until, one day, one of the princes came and seized all the lands in and around the village. The people's appeals to the king came to nothing, nor would the prince listen to any mediation. And so, the people of the countryside decided to launch a revolt against

65

the prince to regain their land. The princess took part in this uprising, helping them, still disguised as a maid.

Once I was finished with the story, the Princess dismissed the other slaves, saying, "Leave us alone." They all left except for Mawahib, who remained in her place without moving, until the Princess ordered, "And you too, Mawahib," and she left with resentment etched on her face.

Once Mawahib had shut the door behind her, the Princess turned to me.

"Is this really one of your grandmother's stories? And were you really on your way to Morocco to bring medicine to your ill mother?"

I was so startled by the Princess's question that I hesitated. Should I tell her my whole story or invent more fictitious tales? Her eyes searched mine for an answer. She had a gentle expression, her face bright with intelligence, and I felt I could trust her, as I had seen her listen to people's grievances with patience and understanding, and she was also an avid reader.

"No, that was not one of my grandmother's stories," I admitted. "And I was not on my way to Morocco for medicine."

I told her my story from the beginning, up until the caravan was attacked by bandits. "And the rest you know, Your Highness."

"That," she said, "is your strangest and most interesting story yet!"

The Princess was silent, as she played with a lock of hair that fell over her forehead. Then she looked at me with a smile.

"We have in this palace a library with thousands of valuable books, and I've long wished to have someone to discuss them with, for none of the slave women know how to read. But you…"

She was silent, and then went to the table beside her bed and took from it a book bound in red leather. My heart jumped.

It was my book, *Wondrous Journeys,* which had been stolen from me, along with the rest of my possessions, while I rode in the caravan! I couldn't restrain myself.

"Where did you get that book?" I asked eagerly.

But I noticed that my words had crossed a line, and I apologized.

"Forgive me, my lady, but this book was with me when the thieves attacked us, and I thought I had lost it forever."

"On the day that I bought you, I bought other things," the Princess said softly. "Your book has come back to you."

"My lady, but it's yours, you bought it, and—"

"It's yours now."

I'm not sure how much time I spent in the Princess's room, talking about this book and the strange places it described. I found that Princess Noor al-Huda and I shared the same wish: to leave the palace and journey around the world. Then we heard a knock at the door, and Mawahib peered in.

"Shall we light the lamps, Your Highness?"

"Very well, Mawahib," the Princess replied. Then she smiled at me with such warmth that I would almost swear it was a smile of friendship.

"See you in the morning."

I nodded, and as I was getting up she reminded me, "Don't forget your book."

She gave it to me, and as I left the room I nearly bumped into Mawahib. Then I went to lay down in my bed, unable to believe what had happened.

So time passed in peace and quiet, and I spent most of my days and nights in the company of Princess Noor. We would go to the palace library and choose from among its many books, reading and discussing them together, and she taught

me to swim and ride horses. She began to call me Ajeeba—
"Wonder"—just as my father's friend Omar once had.

The Princess ordered that I be moved into my own room
beside her rooms, and it was this that Mawahib couldn't stand—
that I moved into a room larger than the one for the other
jawari, where I had been for only about three months. The
new room was large and elegantly furnished, with a window
overlooking the garden.

I grew used to my life in the palace and treasured my
friendship with the Princess, who was an astute reader. But
sometimes, our days were disturbed by the shouts of King
Taqi al-Din: "I told you that red is forbidden today!" Then we
would hear the sound of vases being knocked over. "I told you
white—white, you idiot!"

The slaves in the palace would leap into action, changing
the roses and other flowers from red to white, and then he
would shout, "Where's the Princess Noor al-Huda? I want the
Princess immediately!" The slaves would come, trembling with
fear, to call the Princess, who would take her time in going to
see her brother, her head held high with confidence and pride.
Then she'd return from the King's quarters wearing a weak
smile. "It's one of his spells. He'll be better soon."

Later, she would say to me, "He doesn't want me to listen
to complaints from the people. He says he's a fair ruler, and
anyone who has grievances is a liar and wants to overthrow the
monarchy." Then she would let out a loud sigh. "These stupid
charlatans have completely taken over his mind, and he does
everything that wretched Jabbour asks."

Jabbour's control over the King worried her, she neither knew
how to get rid of him nor how to release her brother from
his grip. Then a new story occupied the Princess, setting off
whispers and rumors throughout the palace. This time, the story

was about Tamayim, who lived in the *jawari* room where I had lived and who, they said, was in a relationship with the head groom. It was said that she carried his child. The punishment for the slave woman and groom would be death by flogging, and, in the palace, speculation began and wagers were placed between slaves and servants over how many lashes Tamayim could endure before she died.

Princess Noor al-Huda summoned the couple to her room, and after a short while they emerged, weeping from happiness and gratitude. She had emancipated them, given them land in a rural part of the country, and provided them means to keep them safely out of sight.

When the King learned the story of the slave woman and the groom, he went mad and shouted, sending for the Princess. We heard them shouting, before the Princess emerged and slammed the door behind her. When I reached her quarters, she ordered everyone out but me.

"This crazy man slapped me! This is the first time he's ever raised a hand against me—he has completely lost his mind!"

Then her voice dissolved into sobs. I tried to calm her, murmuring that what she'd done was right.

"But Jabbour, the charlatan, wants their blood!" the Princess said. "He convinced my brother that if they aren't punished, a disaster will befall the King, so the idiot sent his soldiers to search for them."

She took my hand. "I am frightened for them, my dear Ajeeba. What should I do?"

I held her hands in mine.

"Be patient. If it's God's will that they survive, all the soldiers in the world won't be able to find them."

And indeed, the King's soldiers could find neither the groom nor Tamayim, and after a while the King forgot about them and turned his attention to other things. Jabbour persuaded him to go on a journey to the desert mountains, to seclude and purify himself, and Jabbour prevented the King from taking anyone else.

During the King's absence, the palace was filled with a beautiful peace, and life returned to its previous path. The close friendship that grew between me and Princess Noor al-Huda angered Mawahib, who felt she was losing her standing with the Princess. She tried to destroy this relationship in different ways, spreading it about the palace that I controlled the princess, just as Jabbour controlled the King, and that, like him, I was a powerful sorcerer. Some rumors went even further, alleging that Jabbour and I had formed an alliance in order to take over the palace. When these rumors reached the Princess, she called for Mawahib and warned her to stop spinning this intrigue, or else she would be returned to the slaves' quarters behind the kitchen. Grudgingly, Mawahib fell silent.

The King was gone for months without anyone knowing where he was. In his absence, the Princess governed and dealt with the grievances of the people and running the affairs of the kingdom . Then came the day when a screaming man entered the palace, slapping his head and shouting, "The King is dead! The King is dead!"

The Princess questioned him.

"I was coming back with my sheep after they'd grazed," he said, "and I heard a horse whinny. When I got closer, I found these bloodstained clothes, and among them this cloak, which carries the insignia of the King. I walked four long days to tell you this."

Then he fell to the ground, unconscious.

Immediately, the Princess sent soldiers to the spot the shepherd had described. After weeks of searching, they returned with the horse, but with no trace of the King or Jabbour who was the only one accompanying him on this meditation trip.

A period of mourning was announced in the kingdom, and the people donned black. For a month, the Princess received mourners and continued to manage the affairs of state. After this period of mourning, a delegation of ministers came to ask the Princess that she be crowned Queen of the nation, so that the kingdom's affairs could be governed. And so, she was crowned, and the celebrations lasted an entire week. The country and its people were filled with joy that they were rid of the unjust ruler, and his sister had been crowned in his place. The charlatans had disappeared from the palace as soon as they had heard of the King's death.

Noor al-Huda was now occupied with affairs of state, and it was rare that we had any time to read books together. As Queen, she began to change the unjust laws put in place by her brother. Now women were allowed to walk in the streets, while before they had been prevented from doing so by the King, and she reopened the libraries that had been closed on Jabbour's orders, while also ordering the building of schools, sanatoriums, rest houses, and—at the outskirts of the city—an enormous hospital.

I became her personal adviser, and she turned to me often to discuss laws and rulings, which bothered the Chief Minister. Noor al-Huda ruled for a year, during which time the country saw many changes that helped the people. Then one day, she summoned me to her quarters.

"Some of the state ministers don't believe in a woman's right to rule, and they don't like the changes they see around them. They believe a woman isn't capable of leading, and that my ways will corrupt the people."

"But—" I said.

She interrupted. "I've received word that certain ministers, led by their chief, will depose or even kill me if I refuse to give up my rule, and they will put my young nephew on the throne—under the guardianship of the chief minister." Then she sat, holding her head between her hands. "Their plan is complete, although I don't know when it will be set in motion."

"They can't do that!" I said. "The country has grown in beautiful ways…"

"My destiny has been written," she said, as though she hadn't heard me. "Now I'm waiting, though I don't know what form the end might take. That's why you need to leave the palace for somewhere safe before something happens to me."

I took her hand. "Don't talk like this. You'll live to see your grandchildren's grandchildren."

She patted my hand. "You're a free person, and you must leave Egypt. Keep going toward Morocco—there's a caravan leaving in four days, and I will provide you a guard."

I gripped her hands even more tightly, unable to prevent my tears from flowing.

"I won't leave you…I won't—"

"This is my will and my final wish. I want to die knowing that you're on your way to achieve your dream—our dream."

"But how can I leave you to face your fate alone?" I protested. "I can't. It's impossible to—"

She put a hand to her cheek, wiping away the tears. "Your fate is also written, my friend, and it's to continue your journey and follow your dream. You will travel with the caravan. Now I want to stay alone for a little while."

When I left, I was crying so hard I could barely see in front of me. What a cruel farewell—to leave my friend to face death alone! I was ready to share her fate, yet she'd insisted, with all her remaining strength, that I leave with the caravan, refusing to listen to my arguments and tears and my desire to stay.

She took me in her carriage to the place where the caravan was waiting.

"Fulfill your dreams for my sake," she told me firmly. "Remember me, my dear friend."

As soon as I stepped out of the royal carriage, it turned and sped back toward the palace. I stood there, raising my hand in farewell to a brave Queen and dear friend. I don't know how much time passed before the commander of the guard, who had been ordered to protect the caravan, came and asked me to board my camel.

And so, I set off with another caravan, toward a fate about which I knew nothing, clutching my book to my chest and carrying a gold necklace given to me by my friend, Yasmine.

6
THE TEACHER

"But my daughter, I don't teach women, only men," Sheikh Abu Abdullah al-Faqih said. "I could never…"

"I've come from so far away and suffered so many indignities on my way to Tangier," I persisted. "Don't turn me away."

"But I haven't done this before, nor has anyone else," he said. "It's not acceptable! If women wish to study, they do so in the privacy of their home and not in public."

"Ask me anything that comes to mind. You'll find I'm a good student—please."

When I arrived at the house of the scholar in Tangier, I told him my story, and about my wish to be accepted as his student. But he refused. So I went back to him the following day, and the day after that, and every day for a week I kept knocking on his door, trying to convince him, until finally he gave in to my unwavering insistence.

"Fine. But you will sit behind this curtain, and not a *single noise* from you. None of my students can know of your existence, and if you reveal your presence, or if I hear your voice during the lessons, then our agreement is finished. I don't want anyone to find out that I teach women—is that clear?"

"Perfectly clear, my teacher," I said joyfully.

"Well, go get your things from the khan. You'll live here with my wife, and I don't need any rent except that you help oversee household matters. My wife is ill, and she needs someone to care for her. If anyone asks, you're the new servant. But I'll warn you, my wife can be a bit difficult."

So I moved into the teacher's house, and as for his wife, she wasn't just a bit difficult. She was full of complaints and demands, never satisfied with anything, and she never stopped giving orders and grumbling. But I bore it all so that I could continue to have my lessons from behind the curtain.

Then news arrived from Egypt via a caravan. Queen Noor al-Huda had died when she fell from her boat into the Nile, and her young nephew the prince had been crowned King, under the guardianship of the conniving Chief Minister.

Drowned…she was an excellent swimmer. She taught me how to swim! Drowned, it's not possible…

Although I had expected this fate for my dear friend Noor al-Huda, I cried for days over her death—she'd been the closest person to me since I'd left Um Najmuddin in Jerusalem. I clutched *Wondrous Journeys* to my chest as I slept, remembering the notes we'd made and the discussions we'd had, and how Noor al-Huda would say, "Someday, we will make this journey together," or "One day, I'll throw off this life and leave with you."

You have left me and gone on your own journey, dear Noor. But I will keep you with me wherever I go.

So, I kept on with the master's lessons from behind the curtain, holding my tongue with difficulty, so that it wouldn't get loose and answer one of the questions the students could not. After that, I spent the rest of the day in the service of his capricious wife.

"Go get me oranges from the market, and don't delay!" she'd demand. And when I had gotten back from the market, she'd say, "I lost my appetite for oranges, set them aside." Or she'd say, "Open the window a bit, do you want me to roast?" And then, "Do you want me to die from the cold?"

Whenever she got the chance, she complained about me to Sheikh al-Faqih. "This maid is lazy and doesn't know anything, I want a different one." He would calm her outbursts of anger, promising to find her another maid.

But my teacher was surprised by how quickly I learned, and by the progress I was making in my studies. He said I'd surpassed most of his students in knowledge and intellect, and these few words from the master pleased me greatly.

There were also the rare hours when the teacher's wife released me to walk in the historic city of Tangier. I was amazed to see the intricate mosaics that covered the walls of their public baths, and I was drawn to the covered lanes, which reminded me of the markets in Jerusalem. I would visit bookshops or go down to the seashore to gaze at the waves or watch the sun as it descended in its red robe, entering the blue and dissolving into it. I was reminded of Gaza and the first time I'd seen the sea. *How far you are, Palestine!* I was eager to explore the mysteries of this sea, but didn't know that day was closer than I could have expected.

Life in my teacher's house went quietly and smoothly, and except for his wife's constant complaints, things were well, and I learned to distinguish her important demands from those I could safely ignore. In my classes, I learned at the hands of scholars of law, literature, poetry, science, medicine, and astronomy. And all this time, I held my tongue in check.

Until the day came when my teacher asked his students an astronomy question which they were unable to answer. I knew it, as I'd memorized some of the books and knew them by heart. The other students hesitated. Some gave incorrect answers, while others stayed silent.

"It's clear as day!"

My words just popped out. I'd been unable to hold my tongue any longer. The students gasped when they heard my voice, starting to whisper among themselves, and I clapped a hand over my mouth and ran inside. One meaningless sentence had changed the course of my life forever!

"What have you done, my daughter?" my teacher asked later, as I gathered my clothes and things, preparing to leave his house.

I wept with defeat. "My tongue got away from me, and I…" I burst into tears, and the kind Sheikh put a hand on my shoulder.

"Never mind, you've learned a lot."

"But it isn't enough," I said. "I want more."

"Perhaps it's time to leave, and what happened today is the will of God. Don't be sad." Then, his back bent, he left.

What was I to do now, and where would I go? Should I return to my country? I missed Shams, and her children, and Um Najmuddin… Or should I go back to my forgotten village on the mountain? Why had I left behind a peaceful and predictable life in Palestine to follow a crazy dream? Should I turn back or go ahead? And to where? I loved Tangier, its *Zawaya* and *Takaya*, alleys and religious schools. I loved its good and generous people. I loved its sun, which reminded me of the sun in Palestine, and I loved its sea, its…sea!

Yes—I would travel by sea!

But how? And to where? I began to ask among the ships that lurked at Tangier's shore. I learned that one would sail a week later to Genoa, and I thought, *Well, a city to discover!* When I returned to the inn, I asked how I could register my name as a passenger on the ship. I was surprised when the innkeeper told me it was impossible to travel by sea without a husband or father or brother, and that I would not be allowed on board without a guardian.

A guardian! Where am I going to find a guardian? I've managed to travel this far alone, so what do I need one for now?

I sat in my room at the inn and lamented my ill luck in not being born a man. *If I were a man, I could travel without needing permission or guardianship from anyone!*

Then I thought, *So…why not be a man? That's crazy,* my mind said. But my heart replied, *No, it's not. Since the day I was born, my life hasn't been normal.* I remembered the story I'd invented one day for Um Najmuddin about my mother dressing me in boys' clothes and cutting my hair short to protect me from becoming the property of a prince.

And off to the market I went in a state of intense emotion, as though I'd just discovered the secret of life. Then back to my room, where I cut off my long hair and donned a tight leather shirt that was more like armor, squeezing my chest to hide the signs of my femininity. I put on wide men's trousers and a green silk shirt, and over it a black cloak that fell to my feet. I put a turban on my head and then looked into the mirror. *Do I look like a man? A small one, maybe.* I began to practice moving like a man in front of the mirror—moving more vigorously, using my hands a lot, and sitting with my knees apart.

"What's your name, ya Sayyidi?" I asked myself, trying to roughen my voice, which sounded like a child at the edge of puberty. *"My name is Ajeeb. My name is Ajeeb. Yes, Ajeeb."* I began turning around, to check myself from all sides and see if there was anything that would reveal my secret. And when I believed I'd completely succeeded in transforming into a man, I figured, *"Let's test it."*

I went down to the street and approached a vegetable seller from whom I'd bought produce from before, for the teacher's wife.

"Peace be upon you," I said in a voice I tried to make as rough as possible.

"How can I help you, Sir?" he said.

"I want some apples." I took them and walked away, almost leaping with happiness.

I'll try something harder, I thought, and I went into a fish restaurant. The place was completely packed with men, and there was not even one woman. I sat at a table in the back of the restaurant.

"What shall I bring you, Sir?" the waiter asked, without even looking at me twice.

"Grilled fish with vegetables," I said.

After I ate at the men's restaurant, I walked in the street, tossing out "peace be upon you" left and right, and no man gasped or said, "That's a woman." And I told myself, *I've done it, I've succeeded!* Then I wondered, *Do I dare? Why not!* So I entered a sailors' bar, where the smell of cheap tobacco and drink were so thick I nearly suffocated, and their voices rose, shouting out crude and vulgar words. At one end of the bar, there were two sailors trading punches, and men gathered around them, cheering them on. I grew frightened. *I can't be in here, I can't be a man. What if someone picks a fight? What if…?* I turned to leave and thought of abandoning this mad idea. But as I was leaving, I saw him.

He was sitting at a table near the wall, smoking a pipe and watching the fight from where he sat. He'd put his turban down on the table in front of him, and his long black hair shone in the lamplight. He wasn't just handsome—he was the most beautiful man I'd ever seen. I got closer, attracted by a hidden force that drew me toward him, until I stood in front of his table. But he took no notice, so I cleared my throat.

"What do you want?" he asked without paying me any attention.

I tried to summon my courage.

"I want to sign on as a sailor on the ship that's bound for Genoa. Do you know where I can find her captain?"

He looked me over from head to toe, and I was terrified he would unmask me. His green eyes seared my skin, and I felt blood creeping into my cheeks, until suddenly the man began to laugh. Then he roared with laughter until tears streamed down his cheeks, and he couldn't speak until he'd blown his nose on a handkerchief and put it back in his shirt pocket.

"You want to be a sailor!"

He pointed at me and again began to laugh so loudly he attracted the gazes of sailors all around the bar.

Confused, I answered, "Yes, Sir."

"A child like you will be lost among men! Go back to your mother, boy, and don't come back for another ten years."

And he went on laughing.

I was furious at his arrogance and felt myself trembling.

"I just want to know where the captain is," I said stubbornly. "Can't you show me?"

He gave me a hard look.

"Are you serious about becoming a sailor, boy?"

I felt the blood drain from my face.

"Yes."

"And what do you know about sailing?"

"Nothing," I said. "But I can learn."

"But you're too weak, and you won't be able to tighten the lines."

"I can take care of myself. Where's the captain?"

He leaned back in his seat and gave me a closer look that was not insincere.

"You're talking to him. I'm the captain of the ship—*The Black Angel*."

I took the seat across from him.

"Take me with you, Sir. And if I can't be a sailor, then I can be your servant."

The man gave me a piercing look.

"And why, my boy, are you so determined to ride on the seas? The sea is dangerous. Does your family know?"

"I'm an orphan, Sir, and I have no family."

Then I had another idea.

"When my parents died, my uncle took me in, and he had ten sons and daughters. My uncle was poor, so I went out early to work to help support this large family. I worked as a blacksmith's assistant and a baker's assistant."

He looked at me with some sympathy, so I continued to press for more.

"But my uncle died, and his wife took their children to her family home in the south, and I remained alone."

"Okay, okay," he said, silencing me.

And yet, from the way he said it, I could tell he'd begun to soften.

"But the sea's waters are very difficult, and there are many dangers."

"I'm ready to face them."

"Do you at least know how to swim?"

"Yes," I said with great confidence.

Thank you, Noor al-Huda, my friend!

Then I added, "And I'm the best at riding horseback."

"And where did you learn to ride horses?" he asked with an incredulous smile.

Your tongue, Qamar! When will you learn to shut your mouth? Why do you put yourself in these situations!

"I worked in a stable and helped tend the horses, and sometimes I tried to ride them."

His green eyes locked on mine.

"So then?" he said in a tone not without irony. "What else can you do?"

"A lot of things, I can cook, and—please, Sir, Captain, I want to ride the seas even just once in my life. It's been my dream ever since I first saw the sea. Will you take me?"

"Alright. Come to the ship tomorrow and you can start

work by cleaning my cabin."

I thanked him, almost flying with joy.

"But I won't pay you, understand? I'll feed you for your work—that is, if the fish don't eat you before we arrive in Genoa."

Echoing my thanks, I made to leave.

"What's your name?" he called out to me.

"Ajeeb, Sir. My name is Ajeeb."

When I got back to the inn, I almost couldn't believe it. Here I was, with a chance to sail for the first time ever, and in a real ship with a real captain. And oh, the captain! My face reddened again, and I put my hands against my cheeks and felt the heat radiating off them. *What's going on with you, Qamar?*

In the morning, I went early to the ship and asked for the captain's cabin. When I got there, I heard a lot of comments and jokes, most of them coarse and dirty. The captain entered as I was tidying up his clothes, putting them in in a chest at the foot of his small bed.

"And here you are! Don't forget the back room where you'll sleep," he said, and he went out.

The back room was like a closet or cupboard, and inside there was a mattress on top of some wood and nothing else, with the mattress taking up nearly all the space. It was hard to tell the color of the sheets for all the dirt. This closet would be my home and refuge. Beside that closet was another of the same size with a tub that took up almost the whole space. On the rim of the tub were a few pieces of soap and, beside them, a large brass jug—this must be where the captain bathed.

After I'd finished cleaning the captain's cabin and the two closets, I went out to the back of the ship to ask the captain's permission to leave. He was talking to a few of the sailors, and suddenly I saw one of the sailors head to the edge of the deck and drop his pants to pee in the sea. I was shocked by the sight, which I hadn't expected. I turned my face, which had flushed blood red. The captain noticed.

"You'll have to get used to things like this. You too will learn how to pee that way in front of everyone."

In a stammering voice, I asked for leave and then bolted off the ship and ran to my room at the khan.

Now you've really thrown yourself into a world of trouble, and all your cleverness and knowledge won't bail you out, nor all the world's demons. Better to pull out now, while you're safely on dry land, or this adventure will be your end!

But my sense of adventure said something else. *Every problem has a solution, and you'll discover it if only you try. The world lies open before you, and this opportunity won't come again.* And so, I passed the night between push and pull. One moment I thought I'd return to my country. At another, I took heart and wanted to embark on this journey. I went down to the market, hoping to find an answer to my quandary.

I stayed there for hours, wandering aimlessly, peering into one shop after another. Standing in front of the leatherworker's shop, I watched him cut the leather and sew it with great skill. And there, hanging on the door of his shop were all sorts of leather goods—belts and straps for horse saddles, and bags of various shapes and colors. I stood contemplating the shop and the seller. Then suddenly, I had an idea.

I ran back to the inn, stumbling over my long robe, took out paper and began sketching up plans, then tore them up and crumpled them into a ball.

In the morning, I returned to the leather vendor with my idea clearly drawn. The seller looked at it with great surprise.

"My boy, this is a strange thing, and I've never made its like before. What's it for?"

"Can you make it?" I asked.

"Yes, but…"

"Then make it for me."

"If you told me how you meant to use it, then I—"

"Never mind. Just make what I've got on the paper."

I left the vendor in confusion and went to the market to buy clothes like the ones the sailors wore, and some sheets, and a few bars of soap, and other things I thought I'd need on a long journey. I also bought many herbs for treating different diseases. I returned to the inn with my supplies, eager to try on the belt the leatherworker had made.

I put on the belt, which had a leather tube hanging from it, and stood in front of the mirror in several positions until I could use it like a man. After practicing for a while to master the mechanics, I realized the life of men was never going to be easy for a woman!

I returned to the ship as the sun was setting, entered my closet, and closed the door. I heard the captain as he entered his room, drunkenly singing.

"Hey boy, where are you? What's his name…?"

I came out of my closet and stood in front of him.

"Take off my boots," he said, and he sat on the edge of the bed and thrust a foot at me. After I'd finished, he said, "And my trousers."

Oh, how could I strip a man naked? What a disaster! And now what should I do?

"It's very cold this evening, Sir. Wouldn't you prefer to sleep clothed?"

"Take off my trousers, and I don't want to hear another word."

He was lying on his back on the bed, and he began to snore loudly. So I left his clothes on and covered him with a sheet. Then I went into my closet and closed myself in tight.

I couldn't sleep. The captain's snoring was so loud that the walls of my closet shook, and what's more, I was frightened. What if he found out I was a woman? Even worse—what if the sailors found out I was a woman?

I heard the captain calling, and I went into his room.

"Bring me hot water, quickly."

I took the brass jug and filled it with hot water in the ship's kitchen and came back to find the captain sitting in the bathtub, entirely naked! I left the jug beside the tub and fled the room. The captain called me in a thunderous voice.

"Come on, pour the water on me."

I stood behind him, closed my eyes, and began pouring hot water over his back.

"What are you doing, stupid?"

I opened my eyes to see I was pouring water, but missing the tub.

"This is not a good start, boy," he said angrily. "If you can't handle the work onboard ship , even when we are still at the dock, you can leave."

"I'm sorry, Sir, forgive me, it won't happen again."

"I warn you; I don't stand for laziness or stupidity."

"It won't happen again, Sir, I promise."

"We set sail tomorrow at dawn. There's a whole day for you to think about whether you really want this job."

He stood suddenly in front of me. My face reddened, and I felt beads of sweat sliding down my back. He took the towel, dressed himself, shaved, and went out.

I sat on his bed, trembling. *Do I really want to be here? Can I handle naked men in front of me? What a mess!*

I went back to the market to wander and think, and in the evening I found myself back in front of the ship. So I went into my closet and closed the door tightly. *So be it.* I had made my decision, and when the captain returned drunk, I was ready to take off his boots and trousers.

I woke to sounds of the ship's creaking, and shouts and orders from the crew. Then the ship began to shudder. I left my closet and found the ship was leaving the harbor, just as the sun had begun to appear behind us.

The first few hours passed safely enough, as I stayed out of the sailors' way and busied myself observing the sea and watching them tighten the lines. They raised the sails, and I watched the captain stand at the wheel, tall and handsome. If it weren't for the persistent nausea that cut into my enjoyment, I would have sung with joy.

I went down to my closet and boiled some herbs, after which I started to feel better. One of the sailors shouted, "Where's the new boy? It's time," and I heard the voices of two sailors as they descended the ladder, followed by loud knocking at my door.

"Come on, come on, it's time for your initiation."

"What initiation?"

"Come on and find out."

So. I climbed up on deck to find the sailors standing in a circle, and then the two sailors who had brought me shoved me into the center. And they all shouted in one voice, "Go, go," and one of them said, "Throw him in the water," and another said, "Shave off his hair first," and a third, "First let him drink his jug of wine."

The captain stood at the wheel, looking down on the scene with a sly smile. As for me, I started to shake. *They'll expose me! They'll find out I'm a woman! Think, Qamar, think!* I took the jug of wine, went to the railing, and lifted it to my mouth. Then, with one swift fling, I threw it into the sea.

"What did you do that for, idiot?" someone shouted.

"It slipped from my hands, I couldn't hold on..."

The captain stood in place, his smile growing wider, as two sailors approached me, each grabbing me by a hand and lifting me above the railing. Then all the sailors shouted, "One, two, three!" and they threw me into the sea. And while I knew how to swim, I was paralyzed by the shock and the cold water, and I struggled. Then I saw a rope coming down the side of the boat, and I clung to it. I felt myself rising up out of the water into the air, and then two strong hands gripped me. I stood on the ship's deck, dripping sea water and feeling very miserable. I was about to cry, but realized the two hands that had rescued me belonged to the captain.

"Enough, leave him alone," he said in a commanding tone.

"But we haven't finished the initiation rituals!" one of the sailors said. "Go on, we have to shave off his hair."

"I said enough."

Then the captain looked at me.

"Go and change your clothes."

And I went down to my closet, hardly believing I'd survived.

7

THE BLACK ANGEL

I became used to wearing my leather belt over my chest and wrapped around my waist, so that it became a part of my body. I'd put it on every day at dawn and take it off once I'd tightly shut the door to my closet in the evening. The sailors got used to having me around and didn't bother me, and I began to know some of them by name.

Abdoun was one-eyed, had yellow teeth and a few random wisps of hair, and he smelled of garlic. "Monkey," as they called him, wasn't the name his mother had given him, but it stuck to him until it became the name he called himself. He was so thin that his skin seemed glued onto his bones, but he was quick-limbed and could climb anything with an easeful grace. He often stood in the crow's nest surveilling the seas, for his eyes, they said, were like an eagle's, and despite his great sense of humor he was quick to anger. Monkey was the quickest to wield a dagger and knew the art of using it.

I also got to know the cook, "Cabbage," so-called because he was fat and round, and because he often cooked cabbage in all its different shapes and forms. Cabbage had taken on the task of feeding me because, he said, I was lighter than a feather. Anfara was the ship's first mate and the captain's assistant, who even the strongest sailors feared and avoided, and no one ever saw him smile. Once, I tried to speak to him while he was at the ship's wheel. He answered curtly without once looking at me, and that's when I realized he didn't like to talk and that it was useless to try and converse with him.

After some time, I got used to the motion of the ship and no longer felt nauseous, and I got used to its strong smells, like the reek of rotten fish. I also became more familiar with Captain Alaa al-Deen, who was kind to the sailors and always joked with them, but was also tough, especially when disagreements broke out, which happened a lot. It would start with two sailors trading curses. Then they would trade punches, and in the end Captain Alaa al-Deen would reprimand them, stopping the fights, scolding them, and sending everyone back to their places. The sailors loved him and were ready to die for him.

He was kind to me, even though my face flushed red every time he looked at me. And even though I knew his gentleness was paternal, still, my whole body trembled if, for instance, he put a hand on my shoulder. The captain began to pay attention to my education, and he would walk with me around the deck, pointing out things, telling me their names and how they worked. He was pleased with the speed at which I learned, which encouraged him to tell me more.

Living around these men for only a month, I felt I had known them a long time, as sailors on a ship at sea become a sort of family, talking together, eating together, playing dice, singing, and quarreling for no reason—then becoming friends again. I liked them and treasured their company.

One beautiful morning, I came out of my closet to the sound of shouts and a racket on the ship's deck. When I got up there to see what was going on, Monkey was waving his arms at the horizon, calling out, "Ahoy, there's a ship in the distance," and the sailors leaned over the deck's edge and focused their gazes on a black dot. The captain ordered them to take down the sails and raise the flag. At that moment I realized the ship had been sailing without a flag since we'd left Tangier. Suddenly, when Abdoun pulled the rope and the flag began to rise, I looked at it.

It couldn't be! I rubbed my eyes—perhaps the sun had blurred my vision. Then I looked at it again. *Oh Lord…it's a pirate flag!*

It hadn't occurred to me that I hadn't thought twice when I'd heard the name of the ship was the *Black Angel*. But now I realized that the gentle captain with the green eyes and charming smile was a pirate! *What have you done now, Qamar? You've become one of the thieves of the sea. Fantastic. You get yourself out of one predicament so you can get yourself into a bigger one!*

The captain saw the surprise dawning on my face, and he put a hand on my shoulder, smiling as though he wanted to ease my fears. "Don't worry, we're honorable pirates, " he said and laughed loudly, then turned away and began giving orders to the sailors.

The ship was alive with commotion, with sailors running, each one carrying a sword or a dagger. Some climbed the mast, and some stood at the gunwale, staring at the horizon and brandishing their swords. Others came down into the belly of the ship, and all of them seemed to have forgotten about my existence as I stood where I was, still in a state of shock.

As the other ship approached, we began to see its features more clearly. It was huge and luxurious, and its trimmings showed that it came from a rich country or wealthy traders. Could they see they were about to fall into a pirate's net? If they were able to defeat our crew, then what would happen to me? The captain noticed I was still rooted to the same spot, and he ordered me to go down into the belly of the ship. I tried to refuse, but he shouted, "I told you to go down now!" in a tone I hadn't heard before, and it was enough to make me leap down the stairs.

I closed the door to my closet and sat on my bed, trembling with fear. Then I heard a far-off call, which must have been from the other ship, in a language I didn't know. And after it was repeated several times, a tremendous sound boomed from our ship—the sound of a cannon going off, louder than thunder. I heard a loud thud and wood splitting as the other ship was hit, and then a jumble of our sailors' voices. Among them I could pick out Monkey shouting, "Good shot!"

For several moments, it was quiet, and then I heard a cannonball strike our ship. The sound was so terrifying I thought my ears would explode and my closet would tumble down to the ocean floor. I heard shouting, and a loud, clear voice calling for water to put out the fire. Dreadful sounds followed, and I couldn't count the number of cannon shots, nor distinguish between those fired by our ship and the ones that struck it.

I put my hands over my ears, but that didn't stop the sound of the explosions from rattling my skull, and it didn't stop my closet from juddering after every strike. I began to sweat as another powerful blow hit our ship. This wasn't cannon fire. My God—it was the sound of the two ships colliding! We were all going to sink!

A few moments passed before I heard the sound of sailors shouting and swords clashing. There were shouts of attack and shouts of pain, and others calling for help, all mixed up in my mind so that they turned into loud, meaningless groans, and I realized that sailors from the other ship must be trying to seize ours! They would kill everyone—our sailors, me, the captain! My limbs began to tremble uncontrollably and my heart was pounding.

I don't know how long the fighting continued. I couldn't tell if it was day or night or grasp any sense of time. It was as though ages passed, and I lived and died a thousand times.

Then it was quiet. There was no sound of steel swords, no shouting or sound of feet, no cannon shots, nothing. Had everyone died? What had happened? Would the enemy sailors be coming now to kill me? I clung to the wall. It felt as though the blood had frozen in my veins and, despite my trembling, I was unable to move. Sweat crawled down my back like a slowly writhing snake.

I hadn't imagined things would turn out this way…I saw my mother and father smiling, then Shams carrying her children and waving at me, then Um Najmuddin, Yasmine and Noor al-Huda, my teacher, and Captain Alaa al-Deen. And then I heard the sound of heavy feet on the stairs, and voices growing closer. *They've come! It's the end, Qamar. Say your prayers now, if you remember any!*

The footsteps grew closer, then stopped outside my closet. *They're going to break down the door, drag me out, and cut me to pieces. And if they discover I'm a woman… Give me a quick death. Please God, don't let me suffer!*

Then I heard Captain Alaa al-Deen's voice calling me. I couldn't believe it was him, still alive! I began to weep—from my terrible fear and from my great happiness at hearing the captain's voice.

"Open up, Ajeeb. It's over."

I couldn't stand, so I reached out to lift the latch. The captain stood in the doorway, covered in blood that was on his face and clothes and even his shoes, and when I saw him, my weeping grew louder. I don't know where I got the strength, but I stood and lunged at him, hugging him and crying on his shoulder. The captain slapped my back.

"Get hold of yourself, man!"

Then he stepped back and looked at my face.

"Why are you crying like a woman?"

For a moment, I wanted to say, *I am a woman!... and I love you*. But at the last moment, I stopped myself. I straightened my clothes and wiped off my tears with the back of my hand.

"I thought you'd died," I stammered. "I was afraid that..."

He turned away.

"Pirates like us aren't afraid, no matter what happens, and let that be a lesson to you. Now go up top and find some way to help the others."

And he climbed the stairs.

I reproached myself for my recklessness and for almost revealing myself. I washed my face, then took a deep breath and went up on deck.

The sun was still shining in the sky, and I cupped a hand over my eyes. Once I managed to open them, I couldn't believe what I was seeing! There was a huge gap in the side of the ship where it had been smashed, and pieces of wood were scattered everywhere. It must have happened when the *Black Angel* crashed into the other ship. And there were swords and blood on the deck, and a number of dead I didn't recognize. Some of our wounded sailors were at the sides of the ship, and some lay on the deck, moaning and shouting. It was a terrible scene, as though the gates of hell had been opened.

I felt a strong hand take hold of my ankle and grip it tightly. Then I heard a faint voice that didn't match the strength of the hand. I looked down to see one of our sailors with a long-handled dagger driven into his heart.

"Water," he said. "Water...I need water."

I ran to get water for him, but when I returned, he'd already passed. For a moment I froze in place with terror, and then I reached down, unthinking, and closed his eyes.

Some of our sailors were throwing the dead from the other ship into the sea. That ship was now a speck on the horizon, speeding away.

I looked at the destruction around me. Suddenly, I hurried back down to my closet to get some herbs and clean sheets. I ran to the kitchen and asked the cook to boil some of them and leave another bunch in warm water. Then I instructed the kitchen boy, who was sitting on the ground open-mouthed with shock. "Tear these sheets into strips to make bandages."

I took clean water and began to help the men, whose wounds were from swords or daggers, except for Monkey. Somehow a thin piece of wood had pierced his thigh and come out the back, so that it protruded from both sides.

As I got closer he said, "Help Anfara, he's in bad shape."

Anfara had stretched out his legs and propped his back against a wall. He was bleeding from the stomach, his face pale, and he gave a low moan. I went closer.

"Don't be scared," I said, "I'm going to help you."

He laughed through the gap in his broken upper teeth and extended a weak hand toward me.

"You're going to help me?"

Then he fell onto his side, unconscious. I asked Saadoun, the kitchen boy, to move him onto his back and start cleaning his wounds with the herbal infusion, and then to put gentle pressure on the wound. Meanwhile, I went back to my closet and brought back a needle and thread.

"Hold it well," I told him, and I stitched the wound and bandaged it, and then asked two sailors to carry him to his mattress below decks, away from the scorching sun.

I moved on to another casualty, then to another and another, stitching and snipping and bandaging torn skin, until all my clothes were soaked with blood. I kept on, not noticing that the sun had begun to set, until it became difficult for me to see my needle and thread, and I asked them to come with lamps so I could continue my work.

I pulled the piece of wood from Monkey's thigh and sewed it up, and despite the intense pain, he joked and cursed the whole time. Next, I came upon the son of the chef, Cabbage, who was unconscious, his right eye pouring blood. The poor man had lost his eye from a dagger's blow, and I cleaned it and stitched it and went on working. By now, the sun had started to rise and a new day had dawned. When I finished tending to the last of the wounded I stood up. Suddenly I felt dizzy, and fell.

I opened my eyes to find myself on the captain's bed, and he was gazing at me with concern. I hurried to check myself and was relieved to find myself still fully clothed.

The captain smiled.

"Awake at last. Will your majesty continue to sleep this much?"

I lifted myself up on one elbow.

"…Ali, Ahmed, Anfara, Abdoun…they're okay?"

"Don't worry, all of them are fine, alive thanks to you. The three who died were given a decent burial at sea."

I leaned back again, letting myself relax.

"You did well yesterday."

"Thank you," I said in a faint voice.

"In truth, you were able to save the lives of many of my men. So thank you. Rest now…" He turned and went out, and I could hear the sound of his footsteps on the stairs.

I got out of bed, feeling that I could walk and that my condition was much improved. So I washed up, put on clean clothes, and went to the room where the wounded were being kept. There, I was greeted with affection and gratitude. I replaced bandages, wet down the herbs, and helped some of the men shift positions. I learned from them that the other ship had been a Spanish vessel carrying gold and other valuables for the King of Spain, that there had been bitter fighting after they'd rammed our ship, and that they'd fled before our sailors could reach the gold.

Abdoun extended a wounded hand toward me so that I'd change the dressing, and gestured with his other hand at the rest of the injured men, saying bitterly, "All this, and we got nothing!"

I went up on deck and stood at the rail, watching the sea water and white foam that formed lines in the ship's wake and remembering the events of the past two days. How much had happened and how certain I was that I would die! Then I felt a hand on my shoulder.

"You didn't tell me you knew about practicing medicine, too," the captain said.

I was surprised by his comment, as I'd helped the wounded without thought or hesitation. "I worked as a doctor's assistant and read some of his books on the sly."

"What!" the captain said, surprised. "You can read, too? You really are a wonder." He smiled. "But you need to learn something of the art of fighting."

"Well, Sir, will you teach me?"

"I don't see why not."

Then he left and went to inspect the wounded.

So, I began to have lessons in the art of fighting twice a day—in the morning, at dawn, and in the evening, when the sun's heat had eased.

The sailors who were working to repair the ship sometimes paused to watch us, and they would shout encouragement at me. "Hit him on the right!" "Lift your hand more and don't put so much pressure on the hilt!"

I'd be wielding a heavy sword and slick with sweat, trying, uncertainly, to strike the captain, who held a sword in one hand and rested the other on his waist, effortlessly parrying my blows. The lessons continued, and in time I improved a little. I got used to the sword's weight and learned to grip it firmly, yet without too much pressure on the hilt, and the captain moved to avoid my blows.

After he had recovered, Anfara taught me how to use a bow and arrow, about which I knew a little, as my father had shown me when I was a child. I saw Anfara smile for the first time—he never said thanks to me, yet his gratitude showed in the time he spent teaching me the bow and arrow. I asked him once, "Is Anfara your real name?"

"No," he said. "My name's Abdullah."

"So where did the name Anfara come from?"

"It's a long story, and I'll tell you some day," he said, grinning. "Now, show me how to aim the arrow, and try not to kill any of the sailors."

In his entertaining way, Monkey taught me how to use a dagger to make precision strikes, and how to throw it to hit a target—at least when he wasn't leaping around the ship's masts or watching the horizon. Once, I dared to climb the mast, and I definitely wouldn't do it a second time. Getting up there was much easier than getting down. But the view from above made it all worthwhile, and I found that, up on the mast, Monkey changed from an acrobat into a philosopher—he thought deeply about things and had his own philosophical views.

I stood on the deck, contemplating the sunrise as the sailors went about their daily work of cleaning and repairs. *Well, Qamar,* I said to myself. *You've learned the art of fighting. Is there anything else you'd like to learn?* I listened to their songs and jokes and arguments, feeling for a moment as though they were my only family.

I felt very close to these friends of mine, who were so kind to me, especially after the clash with the other ship and all their injuries. Before this, I'd thought pirates were madmen, and that they'd kill anyone in their path, like the bandits who had attacked our caravan as we traveled from Palestine to Egypt. But now they'd become my friends, and I understood their way of life. I'd discovered that pirates, despite what they did on the ship's deck, were deeply loyal to their own codes and traditions, and that things weren't as chaotic as I'd thought. Working as a pirate wasn't about getting rich quick, it was a way of life. For them, it was worth leaving their family and home and neighbors, and any other sort of work, for a life spent mostly at sea. A pirate wouldn't know if he would ever see land again, and his whole life would be a journey toward an unknown end, full of unrelenting dangers. Oh, what lovely villains they were!

I was still absorbed in these thoughts when I heard Monkey shout, "Land ho!"

Land! The sailors gathered joyfully at the side of the ship, waving at a black dot that had just appeared on the horizon.

"Lower the sails and bring down the flag," the captain said. "We'll enter the city as nice, respectable tradesmen."

The black dot grew nearer, and the sun leaned toward setting.

8
REVELATION

I was sitting with my friend Monkey on the steps of a giant church, underneath its gas lamps, watching as people milled around the square on a warm evening. I watched the clusters of pigeons strutting around the square as though they owned the place, not even bothering to fly off when people approached. Most of the other sailors had gone to the bars to look for a drink and a woman in whose arms they could spend the night. The captain too had disappeared into the bar with a group of sailors, and I'd begun to feel a jealous twinge in my heart. *Maybe the captain is sitting with one of them right now, and his green eyes are studying her charms...*

Monkey interrupted the chain of my thoughts. "Where've you gone, man?"

"I'm still here," I said in a tone that came out as defensive. "Are we going to carry the drunken sailors back to the ship tonight?"

"Forget them," he said. "If they want to go back, they'll find their way."

Silence again fell between us.

Here you are, sitting on the threshold of one of God's great houses in a strange country. How distant Palestine seems! What would the people of our village think if they could see this amazing, beautiful city, with its mix of genders and shapes and colors that none of them could imagine, its people dressed in strange clothes in even stranger colors.

Then Monkey elbowed me. "Look at that masterpiece, that beauty. Glory be to God!"

He was pointing at a woman who was coming our way, and she was indeed very beautiful and graceful, wearing a pink silk dress that cleaved to her body, then fell to her ankles in broad folds. The woman stood in front of us, then suddenly spoke as she looked at me. Monkey began to laugh and struck me on the back.

"This is your night of happiness, my lucky man! This sparrow has fallen into your hands."

Amazed, I asked, "What did she say?"

"She wants to invite you to her house."

Then he winked at her.

"Me?"

I was so surprised, I didn't know what to say.

"Yes, you're the lucky one. If only she'd looked at me…"

I was still stammering from the shock.

"Please thank her for the invitation, but I must go back to the ship for guard duty in a bit."

"Are you crazy? Such a temptation falls into your hands, and you reject it? Are you not a man? How could you refuse such a Godsent gift?"

"Please," I said firmly. "Tell her only what I told you."

Monkey said a lot of things, and I didn't understand any of it, but when he finished his final sentence, the woman slapped him hard on the face, and then she walked away with quick, angry steps.

"Why did she slap you?" I asked.

"Because I told her you didn't want her, but I was ready to go in your place. It's a sin for such a beauty to sleep in a cold bed tonight!"

Then he stood in front of me, showing off his modest muscles.

"Imagine rejecting a man as handsome, strong, and elegant as me!"

"She's missing out," I said, and the two of us burst out laughing. But discussing this lady had made me long to wear a woman's clothes again instead of my coarse robes. *"If I were in her place, I'd go looking for the captain."*

I returned to my closet, expecting the captain to come back to his room. *If only I could tell him! If only I could put on a woman's clothes again, I would tell him everything and show him how much I care for him. Tomorrow, I'll go to the market to buy women's clothes. I'll surprise him tomorrow... I'll put on the clothes and tell him...*

I was in the market, looking at the brightly colored silk dresses, thinking how much I missed the touch of these fabrics against my body, instead of such coarse leather belts.

Then I heard a familiar, beloved voice.

"And who are you buying these beautiful clothes for?"

I grew confused and blushed. I was caught red-handed. Should I confess to him now?

"It's for my sister."

"You didn't tell me you had sisters. I thought you were an only child."

"She's married, and I only see her occasionally, and..."

Then, as if he hadn't heard what I said, "Buy her the red dress, it's beautiful."

And he disappeared among the buyers, sellers, and goods in the large market.

I bought the red dress and carried it to my closet, telling myself, *Tonight, I'll wear the red dress that he chose.* But he didn't come back that night, either, and four days passed that I didn't see him.

He didn't come back to the ship, and I didn't see him in the market, and I didn't find him in the bars that were frequented by sailors. So, I asked Abdoun, "Where's the captain? I haven't seen him for a while."

"You won't see him again before we set off."

"Why?"

"The reason is blonde and has countless charms!" he said as he leapt into the boat that would take him to shore.

So he has a woman! Maybe he's married to her, and he visits her whenever he stops in Genoa. Maybe they have kids. Maybe he has a woman in every port! I won't tell him. I won't be just some woman waiting in one of his ports, who he returns to whenever he's carried there by longing or the sea. I'll stay as I am and bury this love in my heart.

The rest of the week passed, and I swung between fits of intense jealousy and a feeling of hope. *Maybe she's not his wife, and he doesn't love her, and he just wants to have a good time with her.* Then I'd imagine him sitting beside her, looking into her eyes, and holding her hand in his, and I'd swing back to a stinging jealousy that nearly killed me.

Finally, we came to our last day in Genoa. Tomorrow, we'd set sail, and he'd come back alone. He was very busy after he got back to the ship, what with tossing out orders, arranging things, and loading the food, water, and other necessities for another journey. He stood, smoking his pipe, contemplating a sailor who was staggering beneath a big barrel of water, and I thought: I'll tell him now and to hell with the consequences!

"Captain," I said in a quavering voice. "I want to tell you something."

"Not now, not now. Tomorrow. I'm busy."

And he began tossing out a series of orders to the sailors.

I went down to my closet, took out the red dress, and cried. The next day, I heard him shout, "Haul up the anchor, tighten the lines." Slowly, the ship began to move. I went out on deck, my eyes red from tears and sleeplessness, and watched the port move away. The sounds of land began to disappear as we returned to the calm and the sounds of the sea. The sailors were still in a joyful mood, sharing stories about their adventures in Genoa.

I'll tell him this evening, tonight.

That night, I went to my closet and took off my leather belts and put on the red dress. I felt so airy and free without my belts, in this loose dress. Oh how I'd missed being a woman! I let down my hair, which had grown a little longer, and then I looked at my hands, which had become as rough as the hands of the sailors. But no problem—overall, I looked like a woman. In my mind, I began to prepare what I'd say to the captain when he came back to his cabin. I'd tell him I loved him, and that... I heard the sound of footsteps on the stairs, then entering the cabin. After that, the sound of movement in the bathroom.

I'll come out wearing this dress when he tells me to take off his shoes. My heart beat quickly, and I felt the blood rush to my face. *Hold on, hold on, Qamar, now he'll call you, now you'll surprise him.*

"Ajeeb, where are you my friend?"

As he spoke, I became aware of his mood. His temper this evening was calm, and he was ready to listen.

"I'm coming," I answered from behind the door.

I put my hand on the latch, my heart outrunning me, my legs trembling. *The moment has come. I'll throw myself against his chest, I'll kiss his face, I'll...*

At that moment, I heard a loud scream and the sound of feet hurrying down the steps, and Abdoun's voice alerted the captain, "Monkey stabbed Ali in the chest, and he's bleeding!"

"Quickly, Ajeeb!" the captain said.

Then I heard his feet, and Abdoun's, racing up the stairs.

Why, my friend, did you have to choose this particular moment to stab Ali? I didn't give myself time to think. I pulled off the red

105

dress and put on my belts and the rest of my men's clothing and went up on deck. Ali was lying on the ground. Someone had put a sack under his head, and Monkey was being held by two burly sailors. He was spitting blood and shouting at Ali.

"Next time, I'll kill you!"

"Take him away before I lose my temper," the captain said, and the two sailors dragged Monkey by the elbows, taking him down into the belly of the ship. I approached Ali, whose wound wasn't fatal. If Monkey had wanted to kill him, he would be dead. I treated and dressed his wound, and then we brought him down below decks, where I stayed watchful by his side that night.

I must have dozed off, because I woke in horror to someone shouting at the top of his lungs.

"Ship in the distance!"

I got up quickly and saw there was a ship approaching. This time, the captain didn't order me to go down to my closet, but told everyone to get ready, tighten the sails, and raise the flag. When the other ship grew near, we found it was a small one, about the same size as ours. Then I noticed the pirate flag that flew above it, and their sailors and ours began to exchange vile abuse and indecent gestures, so that I didn't understand if they were friends or enemies.

I spotted the captain of the other ship. He had a huge body, a big black beard, and a thick mustache. He cupped his hands over his mouth and shouted to Captain Alaa al-Deen.

"So, Alaa al-Deen, we meet again!"

"Happy to meet you, Captain Sir," Alaa al-Deen shouted. As he spoke, he bowed playfully.

"Then let's see who's the king of the seas," the captain shouted.

At a signal of his hand, the other ship fired a cannon at us, and the shot fell into the sea. The other captain bellowed with laughter, and Alaa al-Deen shouted, "Respond to Captain Jaafar's greeting." Our ship shot a cannon at theirs, and the shot fell into the sea.

"Are we going to fight that ship?" I asked Abdoun, who was standing at my side.

"Of course."

He made a crude hand gesture and spit into the water.

The other ship was very close and getting closer, as we continued to move toward it. If we kept going like this, there was going to be a collision—the two ships would crash! My heart began to hammer with fear. *Will I be able to fight?*

Our sailors threw a rope out onto the other ship and tugged it toward us until the two ships stood close together. Our sailors leapt onto the other ship, and some of their sailors boarded ours. I stood with sword in hand, not knowing exactly what to do. This was a real fight, not practice.

Then, behind me, I heard one of our sailors shout, and I turned to see him clashing with one of the pirates from the other ship. Our sailor's sword hand was bleeding heavily. The sword had slipped from it, and he'd begun to retreat with stumbling steps. The other man raised his sword over his head with both hands, ready to strike. At that moment, without thinking, I attacked quickly, thrusting my sword into the man's chest. It plunged into his heart and he fell. Before I could think about what I was doing, I helped our sailor onto his feet.

"Are you okay?"

"It's nothing, thanks, look out!" he shouted, looking over my shoulder.

I turned to find someone coming toward me, carrying a long sword. The man was huge, with hair that fell to his shoulders and a terrifying smile on his face, looking as though he wanted to drink my blood. As he got near, I lifted my sword, but he knocked it away with one powerful blow. I started to retreat, but he kept coming at me, his sword pointed directly at my heart. He lifted his sword high in his right hand, but then suddenly he pitched forward and crashed down on top of me. Before I fell, I saw Anfara from the corner of my eye, standing in the distance, holding his bow and winking at me—he'd shot an arrow in my attacker's back at just the right moment.

The sailor's body was very heavy, and his smell was making me nauseous. I was still struggling to get out from beneath him when I saw the captain's shoes, and then he pushed the man off me. The captain offered his hand to help me stand up and recover my sword, then with one jump he was on the other ship, back at the fighting. I stood, breathless, watching his graceful movements and how he avoided blows as if he were dancing, and then I felt a heavy blow to my head.

I woke when cold water splashed on my face. I was still lying on the deck, and I opened my eyes, but the sun forced me to close them again. When I tried to raise my head, I felt the ship spin. I lowered it back down and put a palm over my eyes to protect them from the scorching sun. I opened my eyes again to see Cabbage's kind face looking down with concern.

"Thank God you're okay!"

"What happened?" I asked.

When I opened my mouth, I felt a severe pain in the back of my head. I put my hand to the spot and found a lump the size of a small orange.

"Someone hit you on the head with a chest," the cook said, taking my hand to help me sit up.

I touched the lump again, and my head burst with pain, as if someone were continuously striking it with a stick. I looked around, and my dizziness made it seem as if the ship was spinning. But in this glance I managed to spot some of the wounded, and saw that the *Black Angel* didn't seem damaged, and there was no trace of the other ship. I felt the cook put a towel with cold water over my lump, and I took hold of it and kept it in place.

"And the captain, is he alright?"

He smiled reassuringly.

"He's fine, and so are most of the sailors. If you want to help them, help yourself."

He gave my shoulder a fatherly pat and went back to the kitchen.

I was still sitting on the ship's deck, feeling the lump on my head, when the blood-stained captain approached.

"Are you okay?" he asked, smiling.

"Yes," I said. "You?"

"The wounded need you," he said, extending a hand to help me up. "By the way, your defense is still weak."

He left me and walked off. I started to treat the wounded despite the severe pain in my head. Their wounds weren't serious, except for one of the sailors, called Blink, whose hand had been cut off at the wrist. I had to bring some coals and cauterize it, and the smell of burning flesh stirred up my nausea. Fortunately, after the wound was dressed, he passed out, and I went to the railing and vomited into the sea.

That evening, I went up on deck, where calm had returned. I saw Monkey dancing in his crow's nest up atop the mast, and a light breeze wafted the smell of salt into my face. I felt a hand strike my back.

"What do you think of this ring?"

It was Abdoun, stretching out his right hand, with a large gold ring on one of his fingers.

"It's nice."

"It's my booty for today."

"But what happened?" I asked him. "How did the battle end? And what happened to the other ship?"

Abdoun gave a loud laugh.

"They were sent off on their way."

My face showed my confusion, and he went on laughing.

"Captain Jaafar is Captain Alaa al-Deen's brother, and he loves to joke around."

I was shocked. This battle, and the blood that had flowed, and the fighting, and the lump on my head, and the man that I'd killed—had been a joke? I began to tremble. I'd forgotten that, in the heat and shock of the battle, I'd killed a man. I'd become a killer!

"You were a hero today," Abdoun said. "And Khanafar is going to owe you forever. Hey, where are you going?"

I ran below deck, closed myself in my closet, and began to shed bitter tears. I stayed locked in all that day, in a state of continuous turmoil, wracked by feelings of guilt, fear, and revulsion. Then the captain pulled me out of my isolation.

"Come, man, let's see what we can do about your weak defense."

Whenever I'd tried to be alone with the captain, to reveal my secret, something would happen to prevent it, as if every small incident on the ship were fate's way of stopping me from speaking. So, I decided to stay silent, and told myself the chance would appear. Days and months passed, but that opportunity didn't come.

That year, we seized the gold off three ships, and escaped two others without fighting. We stopped in many ports, and I got to know a lot of cities—big and small, friendly and hostile—and I became so immersed in playing the role of a pirate that I almost forgot I was a woman.

The next year, not much happened that was memorable, and I've forgotten most of it. We stole a Dutch ship, and there was enough gold for us to live like kings for the rest of our lives, but I discovered that being a pirate wasn't just about wealth, or gold. It was a way of life—it was about adventure and heading off into the unknown.

I was absorbed by this adventurous life, and I enjoyed it, even though my joy was mixed with fear every time a ship approached us. My fighting skills were immensely improved at both attack and defense, such that I felt I was born to be a "piratesse," and my life back in Palestine became like a dream that had passed and gone. My relationship with nearly all the pirates grew very close, as did my relationship with the captain, who treated me as a friend and companion, and not as a servant. And even though I still loved him, and longed for his love, I thought that if I told him, I would wreck my life on board this ship and surely my friendships with these men.

My past became like a ghost that appeared and disappeared from time to time. But I continued to long for my sister Shams. How her children must have grown! And when I remembered the good lady Um Najmuddin, I wondered, would I yet see her alive? I still grieved for Noor al-Huda, and despite her death, I felt as though she were waiting for me. But this new life had become a part of me, my destiny. And so, I kept on postponing telling the captain my feelings, until that fateful day.

We were in Genoa again, and most of the sailors were out at the bars. As usual, the captain was among them, or perhaps he was with his charming blonde. I'd stayed on board ship, on guard duty, with two of the sailors—I no longer remember their names—after the captain, Abdoun, Monkey, and even Anfara had failed to convince me to go with them.

It was a clear night, and the light of the full moon was reflecting on the sea, such that the sea turned to liquid silver, and a pleasant breeze stroked my face. In those moments, I wanted my hair to be free, breathing in the warm, salty air. One of the sailors sat at the edge of the deck, leaning on a pole and singing in a warm, affectionate voice about love and longing for a beloved. I couldn't stop a tear falling from my eye, nor from feeling my own sense of great longing. Perhaps the time had come, for this yearning was almost bursting from my chest, and the night shone with such luminous stars that I couldn't contain it anymore. *I'll tell him tonight, when he comes back.*

The other sailor stood at the far edge of the deck, smoking his pipe and deep in thought, or perhaps in a meditative state. Then suddenly I saw a boat approaching the ship and heard the sound of paddles madly striking the water, the rower pulling urgently, as if daring the sea to get in his way. There was a lamp on board, but I couldn't recognize the sailors. Then, as the boat got closer, I heard Abdoun's voice shouting.

"Quick, throw down the ropes, the captain's hurt!"

The sailors on board the ship helped Abdoun and Anfara get Captain Alaa al-Deen onto the deck of the ship. The front of his shirt was stained with blood, and I ordered them to take him quickly down to his room, and to wake the cook. They set the captain gently on his bed and stood around him, and I swear I saw a tear fall from Anfara's eye. I tore open his shirt and found an open wound on his chest, near his heart. The captain was unconscious, and blood was still pouring from his chest, and in that instant I realized I might not be able to save him.

I tried to stanch the bleeding, but it wouldn't stop. I washed the wound with disinfectant herbs and placed bandages on top of it, but these were quickly soaked through with blood. I asked Abdoun, who stood stunned beside the captain's head, what had happened.

"There was a fight between the captain and one of the drunken sailors from another ship," he said. "But he was so drunk he could barely hold his sword. The captain struck faster, and he died immediately. Then some of the sailors from the other ship came to attack the captain, so we went to help him, and there was a fierce battle inside the bar. After it was over we found the captain lying on the ground, with his chest slit open!"

Abdoun fell silent, unable to go on, his words choked off by tears. Anfara broke in.

"That whore killed him!"

I looked at him in surprise. "What did you say? But Abdoun just said…"

He went on without looking at me.

"She took advantage of the moment and plunged a knife into his heart after the end of the battle. She was sitting on the ground with the knife in her hand, wailing and howling that, 'If you're not going to be with me, then you'll be with no other woman.'"

"Isn't that beautiful? To be killed by the hand of love instead of by the hand of a pirate?"

The captain's voice was faint and exhausted, as though he was trying to make it sound natural. He had regained consciousness and was trying to sit up, but I ordered him to lie down, and he looked at me.

"You're crying like a woman again."

I changed his bloody bandage and my tears washed down my face. I wept more, falling against his shoulder, sobbing. He lifted a weak hand and patted my back.

"If I don't die from the stabbing, I'll die because you're suffocating me."

I moved away from him, trying to smile through my tears, and then he closed his eyes. I keened, and the sailors gathered closer, and they too were crying. The captain opened his eyes again, staring at nothing in particular, as though he couldn't see. Then he spoke in a whisper.

"What's this funeral? I'm not done yet. A man like me isn't going to die so easy as…"

He closed his eyes, and he didn't open them again.

3

9
SOLITUDE

With the death of Alaa al-Deen, my heart died, and I no longer wanted anything from life. I shut myself in my closet and didn't come out, having lost all desire to go on. Despite the sailors' attempts to draw me out of my isolation, I didn't want to leave, nor to come in contact with anything. My love had died, and since the one I'd loved had died, my taste for life had died with him.

I had made up my mind—I wouldn't go on with the pirate life any longer. Perhaps it was time to return to my country, and perhaps even to my village, where I would live and die in peace. I decided to leave the ship at the first port.

When we arrived in Tangier, I told my friends of my decision. They tried to change my mind, but I was firm. I could no longer bear a life on the sea, as everything reminded me of Alaa al-Deen and increased my sense of loss—the sea, the ship, his empty cabin, the clothes that still carried his smell, and even the sailors' sad faces.

Before I left the ship, Anfara gave me two full bags of gold, saying this was both my share of the booty and the share of Captain Alaa al-Deen. I tried to refuse, but he said that if the captain were alive, that's what he would have wanted. I carried off the two heavy bags, as well as my few possessions. and parted from my friends tearfully, stepping off the ship forever and trying not to look back.

I rented a room at an inn and stayed there, thinking about what to do with my life. I passed hours and days doing nothing but walking aimlessly on the beach. Whenever I saw a ship on the horizon, or anchored at the port, I would flee from that place and from my memories, as on every ship I imagined Alaa al-Deen standing there with his broad smile, waving and calling to me.

After two months of wandering and thinking, I decided to go back to being a woman. So I bought women's clothes, rented a modest house on the beach, and stayed there, deciding what I would do next. I often thought about returning to Palestine, and yet the idea seemed impossibly distant—not only because of the long journey, but because I didn't know what I would do once I got there. The thought of going back to the village gave me chills, as I feared a life of loneliness and isolation. I wondered if I could go back and live with Shams, but even that seemed distant and unrealistic, and I wasn't comfortable with either of these choices. So then what? I couldn't see myself continuing with my journeys and adventures. I was tired of traveling, and my heart was still pained by loss and by memories of the sea. Whenever I thought of traveling, and facing another journey, I was overcome with exhaustion and fear.

At last I made up my mind and decided to stay in Tangier for a while, at least long enough to recover from all that had happened to me. I decided to open a bookshop; this would keep me busy. I needed something to ward off those ghosts that haunted my memories and disturbed my peace. Something to occupy my mind. Books had always been my consolation in dark times. Reading had comforted me when my parents died and when I was held in captivity as a slave. A bookshop would take up a lot of my time—and provide me with a constant supply of books! And so, with the large sum of gold Anfara had given me, I opened a bookhop, the largest in Tangier. I found an honest and sincere young man named Khaled to oversee the business.

I began to settle into my quiet life, coming back to myself and slowly recovering from my wounds, spending time at home on the balcony overlooking the sea, and reading all the new books that came into my hands. After nearly three years, I found the calm I'd been seeking. Tangier became my city, and that balcony overlooking the sea became my place of refuge.

One day, Khaled arrived, saying there was a man who wanted to buy most of the books in the shop, all at once. I was surprised. Who wanted to buy all these books? And why? I instructed him to tell the man that if he was opening a bookshop, he should go somewhere else. But Khaled returned the very next day accompanied by the man himself. So, I invited him out onto the balcony.

The man gave a modest bow.

"Please, Sayyidati, I wish to speak with you."

I offered him a seat and asked my helper, Naila, to bring us water.

Contemplating him, I saw that he seemed to be a very ordinary-looking man, in his early forties, his thick black hair streaked with gray. Yet his black eyes shone with wit, and his teeth were so white that it was clear he took good care of them. His manner of dress suggested wealth, and he sat erect and held himself with confidence. He gently cleared his throat before he began to speak.

"My name is Ahmed al-Maghribi. I am from Kahraman Island. I came to clear up any misunderstandings that may have arisen, as I don't wish to buy the books in order to open a shop."

He looked at me, as though studying me, before continuing.

"I have traveled a great deal, my dear lady. I have visited many countries and cities, had countless adventures, faced death more than once, and through it all I never married. Now, I'm tired of traveling. I want to settle on my small island and live the rest of my days in quiet isolation, among books."

Then he fell silent and reached for his glass of water. After drinking, he held onto the glass and gazed at me. When I didn't answer, he continued.

"I've found that your shop has the best and most valuable books."

I considered his words as he set his empty glass on the table. This man's story was almost identical to mine. And the ending he had chosen was the same as the one I'd chosen—isolation among books. I felt a strong sympathy for him, as though there were hidden ties that bound us. Was it fate or coincidence that brought him to me?

"The store is open for you to choose whichever books you like," I said.

He smiled broadly, then gave a respectful bow.

"Thank you, Sayyidati," he responded.

And he left.

After the man left, I spent some time thinking about him. Had he faced adventures like mine? Had he visited the countries I visited? If we had spoken more, I would have asked him to explain further, or to stay longer. Would I have told him of my own past? I doubt he'd believe it! No one would. Sometimes, when I thought about everything I'd done, I doubted it had really happened. Perhaps it had been a dream, but would I wake from it?

After a period of rebuilding, the store was filled with books once again, and I forgot all about what had happened with the man. Although now, after all these years, I admit that I had begun to feel a sort of attraction to him. I'm not sure what it was that drew me to him. Perhaps it was the similarity of our pasts, or perhaps his quiet smile and self-confidence. But my time was occupied, and I was too busy to think of him. So after a while, I forgot about him and the matter came to an end—or so I thought.

I finished up with all the new books, took care of business at the shop, and went back to my own books on my balcony overlooking the sea. As I try now to remember the details of those months, I cannot, as the days were so alike and passed without event. I remember that, at the time, I felt a great peace and serenity, as if I'd reached the magical formula through which I was content with myself and my lot. Time lost meaning, and even memories of Alaa al-Deen and the sea, which had ripped at my heart, now passed by like ghosts, chilling my body for a moment and then disappearing. They became guests I could conjure at a time of my choosing, and no longer lived with me at every moment as before.

I did nearly the same thing every day, and the only thing that changed was the title of the book I was reading. In a moment of clarity, I considered writing down my notes and committing to paper the stories of all my adventures and travels. But then I changed my mind. Why should I write these memories if there was no one to read them? And if they did, wouldn't they just think they were the ravings of a lonely woman? Or perhaps I didn't write them because I didn't want to relive those bitter moments.

I sent off letters to Shams, imagining that her sons had become young men, and I wrote to Um Najmuddin. Although I didn't know if she was still alive, I often remembered the peaceful times I had spent in her home. In my solitude, I often placed memories of these people before me, which brought back feelings of longing and nostalgia. I would think of Noor al-Huda, and miss our spirited talks and lovely times. But it brought back the pain of loss that I thought had passed, and I would cry as though I had just lost her. *Oh Noor, I traveled as much as I could, and adventured as much as I wanted, and I fulfilled the promise I made to you and to myself. But now I'm tired. Forgive me, Noor, I want to rest.*

The book of *Wondrous Journeys* still hadn't left me, and I caressed its leather binding and turned its pages, written in beautiful script. In those moments, I felt a fever to travel. But this was always followed by the pain of memories, and I would convince myself I had done well to stop and that I was happy with this peace. Then thoughts of traveling would return again, and quickly I would drive them away. And so, my days went by in these echoing circles. Somehow, I managed to find a bit of comfort in the familiar routine, like someone accustomed to their habits who doesn't want to change them.

One beautiful spring morning, my housekeeper Naila stepped out onto the balcony and announced that a man had come wanting to see me. I looked up from my reading to find before me the same man who'd come a year before to buy my books. I don't know how or why, but when I saw him standing before me and looked into his smiling face, my heart started drumming, and I felt a sudden heat in my face.

I greeted him and then asked, "Have you finished reading all those books?"

He smiled.

"I'll need a few more years for that."

I invited him to sit, searching his face for the reason for this visit. His expression told me nothing, but his movements suggested some unease. He drank the juice Naila offered him, smoothed his black mustache, and we exchanged some pleasantries about the sea and the weather this time of year. I don't know what exactly made me feel comfortable with this strange man, as this was only the second time I'd seen him; his first visit had been so short and to the point. And yet, I felt relaxed in his presence, as though his natural place were here, on this balcony, in a chair near me. He was embarrassed when he saw me studying his face, and he said in a low, gentle voice, "I wanted to speak with you, my lady."

Then he looked at my face and fell silent, so I gave him an encouraging smile, and he continued.

"Ever since I saw you the first time, I've been thinking...I mean...I wanted to see you again."

Before I could react to this, he went on quickly.

"I hope my words haven't troubled you, I didn't mean..."

"No, please do continue," I said to him, encouragingly, but I couldn't think of anything else to say.

"I wanted to see you again and speak with you," he repeated, "and here I am. And, for the first time in my life, words fail me."

I gave him a smile I hoped would be heartening.

"I wouldn't think a man like yourself could ever be failed by his words."

At that moment, his attention fell on the table between us, on which sat the book *Wondrous Journeys*.

"May I?" he asked, gesturing toward it.

I nodded.

He took it in his hands and considered it with familiarity.

"This beautiful book," he said, "is what made me start years of journeying and travels. Have you read it yet?"

I wondered at this book, which had brought together my mother and father, and had brought me to Noor al-Huda, and to where I am now. And now, it had connected me to this man! A coincidence? Or was fate still holding something in store for me?

"Yes," I told him. "I've read it."

My expression must have prompted him to say, "And it played a part in your life, too?"

I nodded. He looked at me as though asking me to continue, but at that moment I felt a sort of discomfort. It was as though this man could see what was going on inside me, and suddenly I felt as though I were standing naked before him, so I tried to change the subject.

"Have you come to buy more books?" I asked, laughing.

"No, I came to see you."

And he stared at me intently.

"To see me?"

As he spoke, he continued to look deeply into my eyes.

"I felt, when I first saw you, that we had many things in common, although in truth I don't know what these might be. But whatever it is, I couldn't stop thinking of you. I wanted to call on you several times last year, but I was afraid I wouldn't be welcome."

He looked at me again, as though he wanted to read an answer in my expression, and he must have noticed the redness of my cheeks. I felt confused, and I didn't know what to say. Should I tell him I had thought about him as well, and that I too had wanted to see him again? But instead, I said, "You're welcome. Do you want more juice?"

He answered, as though he hadn't heard me.

"Would you allow me to visit you again?"

"It would be my pleasure."

He stood and reached out to shake my hand, and he held it for a little longer than was necessary.

"Until next time, Sayyidati."

And he left.

Once he'd left, I pressed a hand to my hot face. Do you want more juice? Ugh, you moron! Is that all you could say? What's wrong with you? Why didn't you tell him you wanted to see him, too? Why didn't you react, tell him what was going on in your mind? You want to see him a second time, and a third and a fourth. The man was frank and clear with you, so why couldn't you be the same with him?

All day, I kept blaming myself and my stupid hesitation. What if he thinks you don't want to see him? What if he doesn't come back?

Then I'd try to convince myself I'd done the right thing. Do you want to simply throw yourself at his chest and beg him to come back, just because he said he wanted to see you again?

But…what if he doesn't?

All these ideas kept churning in my head until, the next day, Naila came and announced his arrival. My heart throbbed, and hot blood flooded into my face. With clumsy jerking motions, I arranged my dress and hair. He came in with his confident posture, his warm smile, and those teeth that looked even whiter beneath his black mustache. He reached out his hand to greet me.

"I hope you've still got a bit of juice," he said, and smiled.

"What?" I asked, holding out my hand to meet his, not yet understanding.

"More juice," he said.

We began to laugh so loudly that Naila came running to see what was wrong. I asked her to bring the juice, and we laughed more. It felt as though the barriers between us had broken down, and my feeling of estrangement had completely disappeared as we laughed together like old friends.

I said to him, as I wiped a tear from my eye, "The juice was just my way of avoiding embarrassment."

Then he looked out at the sea. "What do you think of going for a walk along the shore?"

I welcomed the idea, and we stepped down from the balcony and took a pleasant stroll toward the beach. When we reached the sand that was damp from the waves, I kicked off my shoes and raised the hem of my dress without thinking, as I always did when I walked alone on the beach, to feel the cool, soft sand beneath my feet. I gave him an encouraging look, and he slipped off his shoes and lifted the edge of his cloak. We continued walking and talking as though continuing a conversation we'd begun a thousand years before.

We didn't notice the time passing. The sun had begun to set and the sea to turn violet when suddenly he stopped and looked at me.

"I am amazed by how beautiful you are."

I flushed—surprised, and grateful.

After that, nothing more was said, but we continued on our walk until the sea was the color of kohl, and the sky was embroidered with stars that shone like this man's smile. When a cool, gentle breeze lifted my hair, I felt a chill, and I didn't know whether it was from the cold or my situation. Here I was, walking contentedly on the beach with a man it seemed I'd known for ages, and I felt a sense of wonder, as though the stars and the sea had blessed these moments.

He broke the silence.

"The weather's starting to cool a bit. Would you like to go back inside?"

In truth, I didn't. I wanted to walk with this man forever, until time stopped. But I said, "Yes, let's go back."

We started to walk back toward the house, and suddenly his warm hand seized mine in a motion that felt so natural, I responded in kind.

Ahmed's visits continued, as did our seaside conversations, and they were sometimes filled with laughter, and at others, with sadness.

Then one warm morning, he arrived hours ahead of schedule and sat in his usual place on the balcony. He took my hand in both of his and looked up at me.

"It's time for me to return. Will you come with me?"

"Are you proposing marriage?"

"I want to spend the rest of my life with you. Do you accept?"

"Yes," I said without a thought, without even a moment of silence.

Once he had left, I began to think about how I was linking my fate to his, and the idea seemed beautiful and good and true. After all, ever since I'd met him, I had been counting the hours until he would next arrive, and his presence had become an important part of my life. With him, I rediscovered joy and satisfaction. With his gentle touch, he helped me forget the sorrows of the past and unearth the beautiful things inside me. Just his presence made me feel beautiful and intelligent and loved.

We agreed that he would go to his island, and I would join him after putting things in order in Tangier. I immediately decided to give the shop to Khaled, who had served me so well. I invited Naila to come with me, or I told her she could stay behind if she chose. She decided to remain in Tangier, and I gave her a sum to live on. I bought the clothes and accessories I would need, as well as a supply of different herbs, and of course I packed my books. Then I headed west with a small caravan, where a new journey would take me to a man I loved, and to a life of stability and tranquility.

I found him waiting for me eagerly, and he took me in a boat to his big house on the beach, where we were married in a modest ceremony.

Ahmed was a simple and easygoing man, and every day he surprised me with his knowledge and kindness. With him I found tenderness, warmth, comfort, and love. Our daily walks on the beach continued, as did our quiet sessions on the balcony, discussing books and our pasts. We shared stories of maritime adventure, and he was amazed by the fact that I had lived as a man and a pirate for several years. He was especially curious to know the details of that time, and he grieved with me over the death of Alaa al-Deen. Ahmed was a rare and wonderful man. There were only two things that gave me pain and uneasiness: my yearning for Shams and my annoyance with Al Sayyida Fattoum.

Al Sayyida Fattoum was an unmarried woman of advanced age who was a distant relative of my husband's—he had brought her from her village and entrusted her with the housekeeping. From the moment I set foot in the house, she was hostile to me. She interfered in matters large and small, acting as though I had stolen her authority in the house. In this way, she reminded me of Mawahib, Noor al-Huda's slave, and of the teacher's wife in Tangier.

I always found her depressing and gloomy, full of muttered complaints. So, I tried to improve our relationship, attempting to appease her with gifts and by giving her absolute freedom to run the house. But, she went on harassing me, and I did my best to ignore her sarcastic tongue.

I didn't tell Ahmed how she acted toward me. He couldn't make her leave the house, since she had no place to go and only a few relatives in her village. Neither could he reproach or scold her out of respect for her old age. I appreciated his responsibility toward her, so I decided to remain silent and endure.

10
MORNING STAR

Two blissful years in this little heaven passed like a dream with Ahmed. Then, one morning, I woke feeling tired, nauseous, and lacking an appetite. At first, I thought it was because of a change in the weather, or maybe because of the spicy foods Fattoum insisted on making. Or, maybe just normal exhaustion. But when I had the same feeling every day for a week, I realized I was pregnant.

Ahmed almost flew with joy, and tears filled his eyes. Immediately, he went overboard in pampering and watching over me. Fattoum went pale when she heard the news and gave an irritated smile. "Well," she said. "And here I thought she was sterile!"

My pregnancy seemed to take ages, and I couldn't wait until the child was born, and I could carry the baby in my arms. My husband brought a midwife from the city, and she moved into the house during the last month of my pregnancy in case of emergency.

When the time arrived, Ahmed refused Fattoum's and the midwife's orders to leave the room. Instead, he stayed by my side, holding my hand and wiping the sweat from my brow, whispering tender, encouraging words. The more I screamed in the throes of labor, the tighter he squeezed my hand. His face also showed signs of pain and distress, as though he were sharing in my labor. At last, when I felt the pain would tear me apart, I heard the baby's cry—and suddenly I was overwhelmed by exhaustion.

I heard the midwife say, "She's beautiful" and Ahmed say, "Let me hold her a bit," his voice thick, as though he were about to weep with joy. Then I heard Fattoum's voice say, with disapproval, "A girl!" and the sound of her footsteps as she left the room.

Ahmed put the crying child into my arms, and, despite my great exhaustion, the moment I felt her warm body, I knew I now had something precious, which all the world's treasures could not equal. And that this child, with her crying red face and her closed eyes, was the loveliest and most sacred gift.

Ahmed sat beside me and held her little hand. Then he kissed my forehead.

"Thank you for giving me this most wonderful gift. What should we call her?" But before I could answer, he said, "Let's call her Ajeeba, after you."

"Please," I said, "let's give her a happy name. That name reminds me of years of misery and pain."

"Look at her," he said. "She's like a precious jewel or a star shining in the sky! What do you think of naming her Najmat al-Sabah, after the morning star?"

My happiness with Najmat al-Sabah was indescribable in those first moments, and I felt a magical bond had been forged between us, a love like nothing else. It was enough to glance upon this innocent face and those amazing eyes, with their constant look of astonishment, to feel that the worries of the world had melted away. And although Ahmed brought in a wet nurse and a nanny, I refused to let anyone else care for her.

I nursed her and bathed her. I sang her to sleep. I carried her against my chest, talked to her, and walked with her along the beach. Even though she couldn't understand what I was saying, I told her about everything—about my village, my family, and about my pirate life at sea. As I spoke, and as she watched me with her big brown eyes, I could almost swear from the looks she gave me that sometimes she *did* understand what I was saying. Often I found her cradled silently in my arms, listening to the sound of my voice.

Every day of motherhood brought a new joy, and her education overwhelmed me with happiness. In her third month, I surrounded her with pillows, showed her things and told her their names, and she'd open her eyes in surprise and laugh at my movements. It was wondrous to be the one who taught her these first things—her first steps and first words—and who helped her discover the world around her. For me, even the smallest details took on new shapes and meanings.

Ahmed would watch us with a look of unspeakable happiness, and he'd carry her around the house, telling everyone, "This is Najmat al-Sabah, my daughter," as if they hadn't been living alongside her every moment. If he was in the city for a day or two, he'd return laden with gifts and toys and clothes, and when I tried to protest, he'd say, "Our daughter will be a true princess." Every night before she slept, he told her stories and sang to her, and he followed every detail of her daily rituals, from bathing to dressing to meals. Najma was the sun around which we moved, and our daily breath, and her laughter broke the monotony of our days and granted us a pure happiness.

When she was sleeping, we would sit on the balcony overlooking the sea and talk about her, exchanging notes about every movement she'd made and every word she'd uttered. The servants working in the house rushed to carry or pamper or play with her—except for Fattoum, who didn't come near or even smile at her. Najma was afraid of her and ran away whenever she caught a glimpse of Fattoum's face.

When Najma took her first steps, she clung to everything around her so she wouldn't fall. Once, she lost her balance, and there was nothing around to grab hold of except Fattoum's dress—as she, by chance, was standing nearby. "Get your hands off me, they're filthy!" Fattoum shouted. "Look, now my dress is dirty."

Ahmed was in the next room, and he heard Fattoum's furious shouting and Najma's crying. During that whole period, I had been trying to avoid Fattoum and to keep Najma away from her, and that moment was an unfortunate accident. Ahmed came out of the room and lifted Najma into his arms, pressing her to his chest and trying to calm her. He spoke to Fattoum in a cool, calm voice.

"I think it's time for you to visit the village."

Fattoum cried out, weeping and wailing.

"Are you kicking me out, Ahmed!? After I raised you and looked after you, and cared for the household? This stranger has affected your mind!"

"I'm not pushing you out," Ahmed replied, as calmly as he could. "And I'll never forget what you've done for me. But I think you need to go and visit the village for a little while. Your nerves have been strained, and it's been a long time since your last visit."

A week later, Al Sayyida Fattoum was on board a boat, weeping bitterly, looking at Ahmed between her sobs, waiting for him to take back his decision. The ship pulled away, but the specter of Fattoum still hung above it.

After her departure, peace returned to the house, and I felt, for the first time since setting foot in this place, that I was in my own house. Now that I could do as I wished, I repainted the walls in bright colors and changed the old furniture, as the ghost of Sayyida Fattoum hung over every piece. Even the servants became more joyful and lively.

Those were the most beautiful days of my life. I'd carry Najma, or she'd run behind me, holding the edge of my dress as we ran from room to room, playing everywhere. We would discover things together and shout with joy. Ahmed, too, shared these moments with us. He ran with us on the beach, and he made Najma little paper boats that they sent off to sea, Najma pushing them off with her small hand. Or, he would sit on the balcony with Najma in his lap, reading to us from a book or poem.

I knew these days would be the best in my life, and I wished they would slow down. In moments when I was particularly happy, I would suddenly feel as though my heart had stopped beating, as if I was afraid something would come to shatter this joy. Then I convinced myself I was giving too much credence to these unpleasant thoughts, and I'd leap back into my happiness, seizing it with both hands and all my mind and soul.

When Najma turned five, she could walk with confidence, she talked a lot, and she tried to read, flipping the pages, looking at the pictures and trying to name the things she saw. As I watched her, I wondered if she'd be like her mother and grandmother, obsessed with books and journeys. I wasn't sure what I wished for her: to live a quiet and stable life, or to go out and discover the world as I had done? My heart was caught between the two paths. I told myself she'd choose her own way, and I couldn't force her to do anything she didn't want.

Then one day, Ahmed came back from a trip to the city, and he began shouting even before he'd stepped into the house.

"I have a surprise!"

Najma ran to him, wanting to see what it was. He came into the house and took out a small, silk-wrapped package. Najma sat on his knee.

"Open it," he said.

"Is this the surprise?" I asked.

"No," he said, looking at me with a radiant smile. "This is a gift, the surprise will come later."

Najma opened the gift and, with her small hands, took out two golden necklaces, each with a half-shell hanging from it. He said one of the necklaces was for Najma to wear, and he handed the other to me.

"Do you remember the strange shell that we found on the beach? I took it and made two necklaces from it. One for each of you, my dearest and most precious."

"And what's the surprise? Where did you hide it?" Najma asked with excitement.

"What do you think—should we go on a journey together?"

"A journey?" I asked him. "To where?"

"We spend a few days in Tangier, and then we travel on any ship, to anywhere you two want to go," he said. "Don't you feel a longing to travel?"

Before I could answer, he went on.

"I want to show Najma the world. She hasn't been on a ship in her life."

"But she's still little," I protested. "She has her whole life ahead of her to ride on a ship and do many things. I don't think she can manage such a journey while she's still small."

Najma slid down off her father's knee and hugged me.

"Please say yes, Mama. It's going to be a great trip, and I'll ride on a ship. I want to see the city. Please, Mama, say yes."

I looked at Ahmed, hoping to see he'd returned to his senses and changed his mind.

"Please say yes, say yes," he said in the same tone as Najma. There was nothing for me to do.

"So when do we set out on this journey, God willing?"

"In two days," he said.

"Two days? That fast?" I was shocked. "That doesn't give

me enough time to prepare."

"You don't have to prepare anything," Ahmed said. "We'll buy new clothes in Tangier."

And with that, he carried Najma out to the balcony, and I heard him telling her about ships and big cities.

In the two days before we traveled, I tried to convince him that we should stay in Tangier and not ride the seas, and I tried to remind him of the unexpected dangers. But he insisted.

"If she gets used to the sea now, then she won't be scared of it when she grows up."

The two days passed quickly. After a short ride on a boat, we boarded the caravan. Najma rode in front of her father on the camel, and he wrapped one arm around her and guided the camel with the other. All those two days, I was anxious and frightened without knowing why, my heart beating fast, as though I was expecting something bad to happen. I rode on my camel in silence, even when Najma was shouting, "Look, Mama, there's so much sand!" I looked at her, smiling.

We arrived in Tangier at sunset and went down to a khan. The next morning, Najma woke very early and started jumping on the bed and chanting, "Let's go to the city! Let's go, wake up!"

In the city, I forgot my anxieties and fears, and felt refreshed and happy as I watched Najma and saw the joyous surprise on her face as she flitted from one place to the next like a butterfly. Then we went down to the beach, and Ahmed pointed at a huge ship in the port.

"This is our ship," he said, "*Conqueror of the Sea*. It leaves in two days for Andalusia, what do you think?"

"It's great!" I said without thinking.

But the truth was, seeing that ship brought back all my feelings of anxious dread. I shared my fears with Ahmed and tried to persuade him to stay in the city rather than travel the sea, but he was stubborn. Then I tried to convince him to remain in the city for at least a few more days and go on a later ship. But he gestured toward me with a charming smile.

"This is not the woman I know and love! Where's your sense of adventure? Where is my brave fighting woman?"

"The brave fighting woman didn't have a child to fear for."

"Let go of this obsession," he reassured me. "We're just going on a ship for a few days—anyone who heard you would think you'd never ridden the seas in your life."

I hesitated, and he went on, holding my hand.

"Come on, show me your beautiful smile, and let's go eat some fish."

So I took Najma's hand and off we went. I noticed I was squeezing her hand tightly, so I let it go and walked beside her in silence.

Traveling day was quickly upon us, and—comforted by Ahmed's trust and encouragement, as well as Najma's enthusiasm—I set aside my pessimism and fears, and I began to rediscover my own enthusiasm. In truth, my sense of adventure took over. I remembered my feelings of impatient longing at the moment of boarding the ship, as though there were birds flying and twittering in my stomach. So I walked excitedly toward the ship, and when we got on board, Najma began to jump and run everywhere. Ahmed ran behind her, explaining everything she saw or asked about with his usual patience, and I left them and went down to our assigned cabin to unpack our clothes.

An hour later, I started to feel the familiar vibrations of a ship setting sail, the same gentle motions I felt every time a ship began to move, along with the excited tension of heading toward something new. Memories came flooding back to me, and I smiled at the ghost of Captain Alaa al-Deen, who stood before me at his full height with his charming smile.

The first two days passed quickly and easily. Although Najma suffered from bouts of nausea, she quickly overcame it thanks to the herbal infusions I made, and also because she was having so much fun, which left her no time to sit around and be sick. There were too many adventures to be had and things to discover on board a ship. Najma won the admiration of all the travelers and sailors, and I often found her talking to the old cook or sitting with the ship's carpenter, who made her a wooden horse on the third day. She carried it everywhere and kept saying, "It's a present from my friend."

These days passed in quiet grace. The sea was gentle, and the ship swayed over it with agile ease. On the fourth day, a wind began as a gentle breeze and then picked up, so that the ship began to pitch, which brought back Najma's nausea. From my previous experience, there was nothing to worry about—the wind was moving normally for this time of year, and I was confident the ship would not be affected much, as this one was a lot bigger than the *Black Angel*. This ship was more durable, although less capable of evasive maneuvers because of its size. But there was no need for maneuvers, as we wouldn't be getting into any battles at sea.

That night when we went to sleep, we put Najma between us on the bed so she would feel safe. But I remained alert, calculating the speed and direction of the wind from the motion and rocking of the ship. I noticed that the wind had begun to pick up, so I impulsively put on my clothes and went up on deck, just as I would've done on the *Black Angel*. Everything was enveloped in a thick fog, and I could scarcely see the light of the lamps. The ship was pitching harder and I could barely stay on my feet. I approached the captain, who had dined at our table the night before. He was busy tossing out orders and watching the horizon. I asked if he needed any help.

"Please, go back to your cabin, my lady," he said. "Your presence here puts you at risk. Please, hurry back." Then he added confidently, "There's no need to be afraid. We're in control of the situation."

But I could hear the worry and strain in his voice. I realized that I had forgotten I was now a lady traveling with a husband and a daughter—I wasn't a pirate, and I wasn't meant to be on deck.

As I headed back toward the cabin, the sky let loose a heavy rain. Now I recognized the danger, and I tried to move toward the stairs, but my progress was slow because of the force of the wind and rain, and the almost total lack of visibility. Then I heard the sound of a blow and a scream, and I turned and went back the way I came.

I found one of the sailors lying on the deck, bleeding profusely from his head. He'd been struck by a piece of wood that had come loose from the mast, blown by the strong wind. I went to him and tried to help him stand, but I found that he'd passed out. So I took his hands and tried to pull him toward the stairs, or anywhere protected from the wind and rain. But the man was huge, and his body was very heavy, and while I pulled with all my strength, the weight of his body resisted me. Then suddenly, pulling him was easier and his body became light. I saw that Ahmed had taken the man by the feet and was helping to push him. So I shouted, trying to raise my voice over the sound of the wind and rain.

"Let's pull him next to this crate."

We pushed the man's back against the crate, and I pulled off my shawl and started using it to bandage his head. Then I asked Ahmed, "Where's our daughter?"

"She's sleeping," he said.

"Please don't leave her alone, I'll come right after you."

Hesitantly, he walked to the stairs, and then he called to me as he tried to stay standing: "But…you?"

"I'm fine! I'll bandage the man's head and be right after you."

After Ahmed disappeared from sight, I went back to dressing the man's head wound. Then I noticed that he'd passed from life, so I stood and headed for the door that led to the stairs, gripping anything I could take hold of so the wind wouldn't blow me off the ship's deck.

The wind had grown fierce, and the rain was coming down hard—I never knew that the sky held this much water and could drop it all at once. Huge waves were rising up and striking the side of the ship, which was rocking violently. Something was wrong. According to my knowledge and calculations, a wind like this shouldn't be blowing until two months from now. I lost my ability to concentrate—I shouldn't be thinking about the wind patterns now. I just needed to get down to the cabin, to hold onto something so I wouldn't fall. In my head, I had one goal: to get to my daughter and be by her side, as she must've woken up among all these loud, frightening noises.

But the wind was so hard! The rain was striking my face and chest like a knife, and it obscured everything in front of me. Then, behind me, I heard the sound of something crashing, and I lifted my eyes to see the shadow of the mast tilt sharply. The mast was going to fall!

The sail began to tear, as though trying to break free, and I heard the sound of wood shattering so loud that I heard it clearly above the howling of the wind. When the mast began to fall, slowly at first, and then picking up speed, I looked around quickly to find a place to hide. I floundered, unable to see, and then my feet got tangled up in a rope, and I couldn't get free. I fell to the ground, struggling to get loose as I yelled, calling for Ahmed and begging for someone to help me. But my voice was weak, and it disappeared into the sounds of the wind and rain. I tried to crawl in the direction of the crate the sailor lay against. But then something hit me, and after that…darkness.

I woke to a sharp pain in the back of my head, a terrible thirst, and something like a fire burning my face. I opened my eyes with difficulty, but the light stabbed at them, and I shut them again immediately. And my feet felt cold… *Where was I? Was I dead?* Again, I tried to open my eyes, but the light made them feel as though someone had poured salt on them this stopped me from opening them. I tried to raise my hand to wipe my eyes, but I couldn't move it.

Bit by bit, very slowly, I regained my senses. Keeping my eyes shut, I examined myself. My feet were in the water, as was most of my body. My chest was pressed against a large wooden pole, and my arms were tightly bound, a rope wound around them. It seemed I was in the water—the sea! My arms were numb, and my head hurt where I'd been struck hard. I opened my eyes halfway and saw the sea. I turned my head to the right and the left, and there, again, was the sea.

I still couldn't understand what was going on—maybe I was dreaming, or hallucinating because of the blow to my head. Maybe it was a fever, and I was just imagining that I was floating on a piece of wood in the middle of the sea. Maybe it was a nightmare, and soon I would wake up. I would sleep a little, wake up, and everything would be alright. But my arms hurt. If it were a dream, I should be able to move my arms. But when I tried to pull at them, the rope that bound them kept me from moving.

My mother used to tell me that pain feels real in dreams. My mother would wake me soon.

I started to move my fingers to get the blood moving.

I thought if I opened my eyes completely, I'd wake up, so I forced my eyes to open. But the sea was still there before me, and the sun's rays bounced off the water and stabbed into my eyes, sharp as razors. Could it be that this was not a dream?

I tried to remember, and I remembered the wind and the rain and the man who had died, the mast crashing down, and then... Oh God, where was the ship! Ignoring the sting, I opened my eyes wide and looked around me—nothing but sea! Where was the ship? Where were Ahmed and Najma? Where was I? I tried to remember how I'd gotten here—had someone put me on this plank and lashed my arms to it? And oh, the water was cold, and I was so thirsty! I wanted water, one drop of water, and I screamed until my throat hurt and the pain in my head was unbearable, but I couldn't get off the wood to feel the place where it hurt. Think, think, what could have happened? Did the ship sink? It wasn't possible! Another ship must have come to help. This part of the sea was full of ships. They must've found help, and Ahmed and Najma must be wondering where I was. Was I the only one swept into the sea? I thought there must've been others, and I started to yell.

"Is anybody there!"

Nothing but silence and water and blue—blue water blurring with a blue sky.

How long had I been here? They must be looking for me! I tried to raise myself up on the plank so I could lie on it lengthwise, holding it between my hands. After several attempts, I was able to lift up my body, remove the rope from around my arms, and spread out on the wood, gripping it with my arms and legs. I felt a wave of exhaustion and wanted to sleep. I didn't want to think about anything, I just wanted to sleep and wake up when this nightmare was over.

I tried to sleep, but my position on the log was painful, and I was afraid of falling asleep and dropping off into the water...

water… I was so terribly thirsty. I stretched out my tongue to feel my lips, and I felt a stab of pain from the cracks in my skin.

Night fell. I don't know how long I was gone, but when I woke, the world had sunk into blackness, and there was an enormous moon in the sky. I'd never seen the moon look so large in my life. It seemed as though, if I reached out a hand, I could grab it. Its light reflected on the water, and I was floating over a sea turned to silver.

I still felt an overwhelming thirst. Would I die here, on this vast sea? If I didn't die of thirst or hunger, I might drown. And if I could somehow keep clinging to this piece of wood, wouldn't the sharks eventually eat me? Oh God, *let me go quickly, I can't bear much more. Just give me a drop of water and let me die, let me die quickly. These agonies have sapped my strength!*

Then I fell into a darker darkness.

Was this really fresh water, or was I hallucinating again? Perhaps I'd died and gone to heaven, and I was drinking water! But I really did feel fresh water on my lips—I wanted more water, more water please, I was still thirsty. I heard sounds of concern around me, but I didn't want to open my eyes, as this was bound to be more delirium. Then I felt a hand on my forehead and drops of water running past my lips, and I opened my mouth and stuck out my tongue to catch more.

I opened my eyes and saw a woman staring intently at me, holding a cup of water. I lifted my hand and grasped the cup firmly, afraid that she might take it away, and I drank it in a single gulp. I lay back down, and then suddenly I became aware of my surroundings—I looked up and saw a ceiling, not the sky. It had a thatch roof, and light shone through. So, I wasn't floating on the sea, I was on a dry mattress! I sat up on the bed, looking around: a small room with walls made of reeds, no furniture except the mattress on which I rested, and a chest in the corner that was also made of reeds. The room's floor was covered in sand.

I looked at the woman who sat beside me. She was wearing simple clothes: cotton trousers and a long brown shirt with slits at either side. Her head was wrapped in a brown scarf. She smiled when I looked at her, and her teeth were white. She spoke a few words, but I didn't understand them. She might have been speaking Spanish, I didn't know, so she repeated what she said and nudged me gently, urging me to lie back down to rest.

"Where am I?" I asked her. "And what is this place?"

But she replied in her own language and then went out.

Moments later, the face of a child appeared at the door. The shaggy-haired child was wearing a shirt and long trousers. He looked at me with surprise, his eyes wide with curiosity, as though he were examining a strange object. I gestured to him to come closer, and he gave a shy smile and fled. He was around the same age as Najma, and I began to cry. Had I lost my beloved daughter and my husband? Were they okay? Had the ship sunk? How was I going to find out what had happened to them? I had to find out *something,* so I got out of bed and headed for the door. But I felt faint and collapsed. The woman who'd brought me the water came running back, and as she helped me back onto the bed, she said something softly to me in her language.

When I settled back on the bed, I realized that the dress I was wearing when the ship was sinking was folded neatly beside the mattress. My hand flew to my throat, to be sure the half-shell necklace Ahmed had given me hadn't fallen off. When I found it there, still around my neck, I remembered that Najma was wearing the shell's other half, and again I wept.

"Did any of you see a ship sink?" I asked the woman. "Or did you see a ship pass by here? Were there survivors? Please, do you know anything?"

The woman didn't understand what I was saying. But she gave me a pitying look and left the room, coming back a little later with a bowl of soup that smelled of fish, offering it to me. I was hungry but didn't want to eat. She pressed it on me, insisting. I tried to drink a little soup but then handed back the bowl, which she took and went out. Then the world began to dissolve into darkness, and the light that had slipped in through the roof disappeared.

The woman returned, carrying an oil lamp, which she hung from the ceiling with a rope. Moments later, a young man entered the hut along with a bent, gray-haired, slow-moving old man, each of them dressed in trousers and cotton shirts.

The young man stayed by the door, watching me, as the elder approached. His face was creased with wrinkles, which were further exaggerated by the lamplight. He sat on my bed, took my hand, and looked closely at my face. Then he cupped a hand to my forehead, just as a father might do with a sick daughter. He said a few words to the woman, and I noticed he was nearly toothless. The woman shook her head, and the man began to speak to me, talking for a long time without me understanding a word of it. Trying to explain myself with hand gestures, I said, "Did a ship pass by here? Did you hear anything about a ship sinking?"

But he just raised his hands in the air, said something, and walked out, followed by the young man. The woman took the lamp that she'd brought in, leaving me to sleep.

I tried to sleep, but whenever I dropped off, I had terrifying dreams—a shipwreck, Najma screaming and calling to me—so I stayed awake, crying until morning came.

The woman came in and reached out her hand to help me stand up. I stood and went with her. It was bright outside, and I shaded my eyes with a hand as I looked around. There was the cottage where I'd slept and a handful of others like it on the shore, as well as some small boats anchored there. A few fishermen were mending their nets, and I saw the old man who had visited me the night before and the same young man. They walked up to me, the old man pointing to a dense line of trees around us, gesturing for me to follow.

We walked a long time on a narrow, winding path that wove between banana trees and long grasses, some as high as my shoulder. We walked slowly and silently, and the old man often stopped to rest. Then suddenly, the path ended at the edge of a small village, and we passed a few humble, gloomy-looking shops, where people sat on the floor or on low chairs, everyone staring at me with curiosity. Some women stopped on the path, green banana baskets on their heads, and stared at me until we passed by. Finally, we came to a tidy clearing, where we stood in front of a house that was the largest I'd seen in the village. It was surrounded by flowers of all colors and had a large wooden door.

The old man rapped on the door with his cane, and it was opened by a girl of about ten. The old man spoke to her a little and then she went inside, leaving the door open behind her. I looked inside to find a courtyard with a pool of water, surrounded by a few chairs. An old man came out, about the same age as the elder who was with me. This man had a woolen shawl over his shoulders, and the two of them spoke. Then, the owner of the house gestured that we should come in, and when we were seated, he called to the girl who'd disappeared through a door on the other side of the courtyard. The young man who was with us said something to our host, who listened to him and shook his head as he looked at me, and then our host looked at me and asked in Arabic, "Do you speak Arabic?"

"Thank God," I said, grateful to find someone who could understand me. I quickly explained about the ship, asking if he knew whether it had survived or sunk. I spoke so rapidly that the man gestured for me to stop.

"Speak slowly please," he said, "or I can't follow."

Slowly, I told him about the ship and the storm, and how I had found myself in the sea, and I asked if he'd heard of a ship sinking or washing up nearby. I told him that my husband and daughter had been with me, and then I couldn't finish my story, because I began to cry. The old man patted my hand and translated what I'd said for the others, and I went on crying, unable to stop.

The girl entered with cups of something to drink, and the man handed me a cup and said, "Drink this and try to calm yourself so we can speak."

I took the cup in both hands and drank a little. It tasted like hot water mixed with honey, with a familiar, comforting drop of rose water. Still sobbing, I asked again, "Did a ship pass by here? Its mast was broken—did you hear of a ship sinking?" And I described the ship that I had been aboard.

"There aren't many ships that pass by here," he replied. "And if they pass, they don't stop. This is a very small island, my dear, and Malaga isn't far off. The ships stop there."

"So I'm not too far from my country. Can you please help me to go back to Tangier? Please help me."

"Finish your drink, my dear," the man said kindly. "And then we'll think together."

I relaxed a little, knowing I was so close to Tangier, and I felt somehow that Ahmed and Najma must be okay. They must've gone back to Tangier, and they'd be waiting for me there—they *must* be looking for me. The man began to ask me about myself and my husband. He wanted to know details, and I answered him as much as my grief would allow. Then I asked how he'd come to know Arabic, and he said he had lived in Malaga for many years as a young sailor.

I spent that night at the man's house, and, in the morning, we found a small boat bound for Malaga. From there, I'd be able to get another ship to Gibraltar, and from there to Tangier.

11
THE SEARCH

The moment I landed in Tangier and stepped down into the port, I immediately began asking about *Conqueror of the Sea*, which had left for Andalusia about a month before. But I could find no one who knew of its fate. I had begun to feel hopeless when I heard a man's voice behind me, asking, "*Conqueror of the Sea?*"

I turned to find a sailor sitting on a wooden crate, gripping a small *oud* and plucking at its strings.

"I've heard that the ship sank."

"It can't be," I moaned.

The man continued as though he hadn't noticed my distress.

"I heard that a pirate ship managed to rescue some survivors."

I stepped closer to him. "Please, was there a man and his daughter among them? A girl of about five, named Najma, wearing a shell necklace just like this one?"

I showed him my necklace.

"I don't know," the man said. "All I heard was the ship sank and some of the survivors were picked up by pirates, who plan to sell them as slaves."

"Slaves! Oh, please try to remember where they took them, please help me. I have to know what's happened to my daughter and my husband," I said, beginning to cry.

Moved, the man replied, "By God, I only know what I told y—"

"But do you know where they've taken them? Was my daughter with them?"

"Believe me, I don't know anything else."

I left the man, not knowing what to do or where to go. Then I remembered the bar where I'd first met Alaa al-Deen, so I found my way there. But I didn't go in, as women weren't allowed. I stood at the door, and out came a sailor looking very drunk.

"Please, Sir," I asked him desperately, "do you know anything about the ship *Conqueror of the Sea*?"

He seemed to be in such a state of drunkenness he couldn't understand what I was saying, but he grabbed at me, staggering.

"I know something about *Conqueror of Men*, just come with me to the inn, and I'll pay you well."

He smelled foul and was so drunk I could barely understand what he was saying. Yet despite his drunkenness, he gripped my hand tightly.

"Please let me go," I said. "I'm not one of those women. I just want to know where my daughter is."

I had to get rid of him, but he kept holding onto my hand, tightening his grip and trying to pull me toward him. I had to defend myself and hit him hard on the nose, then kicked him in the knee so that he tumbled to the ground—just the way my friend Monkey had taught me in our pirate days. Then, from behind me, I heard a man say, "You fight pretty well for a woman!"

I turned to find a sailor behind me, arms crossed over his chest, leaning against the door of the bar.

"He thought that I was…! But I am a respectable woman."

"And what's a respectable woman doing in front of a bar?"

"I want to know the fate of the ship, *Conqueror of the Sea*. I heard that it sank—do you know anything?"

"*Conqueror of the Sea*... Yes, I heard something like that. I heard that it crashed, and that a pirate ship rescued some of the survivors."

"Please, I beg you to tell me what happened to them. The survivors, where did they go? I beg you. My daughter and my husband..."

I started to weep again, and he seemed to feel sympathy for my situation.

"Calm yourself, my lady. I don't know, but I'll ask about them. I'll meet you tomorrow, at this time, and God willing I'll have the information. But pardon me, you've got to leave now. It's not right for you to stand in front of bars."

"Thank you," I said. "My husband's name is Ahmed al-Maghrabi, and my daughter's Najma. She's wearing a necklace like this one, and on the left side of her neck, there's a birth mark that looks like a berry, and—"

"Okay, I'll do what I can. But please go now, and I'd advise you not to come here again. What inn are you staying at?"

I gave him the name of the inn where I'd been staying with Ahmed and Najma before our ill-fated journey.

I went to the inn, where the owner welcomed me and gave me food and a clean room. The next morning, I went to visit my old bookshop that I'd given to Khaled, the young man who'd been its manager. He greeted me warmly and lent me some dinars to buy new clothes, so that I could replace the torn and dirty dress I was wearing.

I returned to the inn, and when I changed my clothes I realized I was in bad shape. It was no wonder the drunkard had such thoughts about me. For hours, I sat waiting in my room, until it came time for my appointment with the sailor, who I hoped would bring good news. When I lost patience, I spent the rest of the time with the owners of the inn, who knew my story and had expressed great sympathy, even offering me money to help me sort things out until I found Ahmed or returned home. I thanked them warmly, but declined their kind offer. Then I looked up and saw the sailor gazing at me.

"I see you're doing better now, my lady."

"What did you find out?" I asked him. "Did you learn anything?"

"*Conqueror of the Sea* in fact went down. The winds proved too much, even for a ship such as she, although such winds at this time of the year are very strange!" He sighed. "In any case, the ship sank."

"And the survivors, who are they? Do you know?"

"I couldn't find out the names of the survivors," he said. "In truth, nobody knew who they were. That one-eyed Habis, the pirate, was near the wreckage, and he captured some of them. He sold them to some slave traders as soon as he got to the city."

"Slave traders—I must go to them!"

"Wait," he said. "I went to the slave traders and gave them the descriptions of your husband and daughter. But they didn't remember anyone like that. All they said was there were men, women, and children among them."

"Where are they? Where do I find them? Tell me."

"Unfortunately," he said sadly, "they were sold to traders on their way to Egypt."

"Egypt, my God! So fast!"

"It happened that there was a caravan headed for Egypt about to leave, and one of the merchants bought them and left with them."

"When did the caravan leave for Egypt?"

"About a week ago," he said.

"Then I will follow them."

I turned to the owner of the inn.

"Do you know when the next caravan leaves for Egypt?"

"In two weeks—a caravan is heading off on to Mecca."

"That's too late. I'll never be able to catch up with them. Isn't there one leaving before that? Please ask for me!"

"But you know that the caravans run almost every month, and that's quite often," the owner of the inn said. "In some other areas, a caravan sets off only once every six months."

"I know." I sighed. "But two weeks . . . ."

I thanked the sailor for helping me and returned to my room.

How could I be patient for two whole weeks, with the other caravan three weeks ahead of me? I decided to go back to our house and prepare.

The house without Ahmed and Najma was bleak and spiritless, and I expected at any moment for Najma to pop out and surprise me, like she did when we played hide-and-seek. But she didn't appear, and there was no sound of Ahmed's voice.

I got my belongings together for the trip and spoke with the servants about what to do in case of a long absence.

Finally, I joined the caravan headed for Egypt. I kept apart from the rest of the passengers, as I felt no desire to join in their conversations or become a part of their groups. All I could think about was the fate of Ahmed and Najma, wondering if I'd reach them before it was too late. I felt certain I could find them, and that we would be reunited. I refused to think of any other possibility, as the hope that they'd survived and that I would meet with them again was the only thing that made me stay strong through this difficult journey—the only hope that kept me alive.

Some of the women invited me to share in their food and conversation, but I declined gently, preferring to remain alone with my thoughts and fears and hopes. The movement of the camel was tedious and monotonous, and the desert seemed endless.

How many bitter sorrows I had to endure! The isolation in our village, the death of my parents, being far away from Shams and her children, the death of Noor al-Huda—and then the death of Alaa al-Deen, my first love…

But this sorrow was completely different, and I never knew that a person could live with such a tremendous burden of grief, which tore at the heart every moment.

One evening, as I ate my food alone as usual, apart from the rest of the caravan's travelers, an elderly woman approached and sat beside me. She remained silent for a long time, and I offered her a brief welcome.

"What's wrong with you, child?" she said. "Why are you so solitary?"

Trying not to offend her, I said, "Please forgive me, but I don't feel much desire for talk or companionship."

"You carry a great grief, that's clear. But don't you think it would help if you shared it with others?"

"I don't think so," I said. "But thank you for sitting with me."

Tenderly, she put her hand over mine.

"Come sit with us. When a person is alone, their pain multiplies by a hundredfold, believe me."

I tried to evade her invitation, but she grabbed my hand and tried to lift me up.

"But…" I said.

"No buts," she said stubbornly. "Up now, I won't accept no for an answer."

I was loath to leave my isolation, but the woman was insistent. So, I walked with her, reluctantly, and we came to a group of women gathered around a fire. When we got to the circle, the women stopped talking and looked at me curiously. Then one moved to make a place beside her, saying, "Please, sit."

I felt a pressure at my back—the elderly woman was encouraging me to sit—so I sat in the empty space and offered my greetings, and the women responded with one voice. After that, they fell silent, until one cleared her throat before speaking.

"Are you traveling alone?" she asked rudely.

"Yes," I replied and stared at the fire, trying to avoid other questions.

"And what…?" another woman asked.

I gave the elderly woman sitting beside me a look of distress, and she understood.

"Don't bother her with questions. She came to sit and share our company."

The women were silent for a moment before they went back to talking about different matters. One said, "My back is really aching from riding on this camel."

"Me too," said another. "And when it's time for us to rest, I can't feel my feet."

"If we weren't going to visit the house of God at the end of this," a third added, "I would never have come on this tiresome journey—I'd have stayed in my house."

"Truth is," the first woman said, "the visit to God's house is worth it. Imagine yourself circling the Ka'aba and you'll forget your fatigue."

"Oh yes, a pilgrimage to the house of God, it's…."

But I didn't catch the rest of the sentence, as my attention had turned to the conversation among the men around the nearby fire. They were talking about the boy-king of Egypt, and how the Grand Wazir ran the kingdom as he liked. And I thought, *May God have mercy on you, Noor al-Huda. It's just as you expected.*

Another man joined the conversation, saying, "And he buys everything that's expensive and precious from the King's own funds. I heard he bought a ruby as large as a fig—imagine how much that would cost!"

"How much did it cost the boy-king?"

"Instead, you should ask how much it cost the poor people of the realm."

"It's said he has more slaves than King Taqi al-Deen."

I wondered, *Will my husband and daughter end up in the King's palace? That would be an ironic twist of fate!* Then I felt a light slap on my hand, from the lady who sat beside me.

"You went far away. I was asking if you were going on the pilgrimage?"

"Yes, yes," I said, without thinking, as I kept trying to hear what the men were saying. But the woman sitting beside me spoke loudly and drummed on my hand with every phrase, and after a seeming eternity had passed, I pleaded exhaustion and withdrew.

I don't remember much about those days in the caravan, as I rushed to reach Egypt, except that they went slowly and were dull. But when you have to walk through the desert in such a large caravan, it is bound to take a long time.

We had nearly reached an oasis, and the leader of the caravan had ordered us to prepare to dismount and rest, when we saw a thick cloud of dust on the horizon. An atmosphere of anticipation hovered over us. This could be another caravan or a gang of bandits. We waited in fearful vigilance until the caravan leader assured us, "It's another caravan. It must be a big one to raise that much dust!"

The other caravan approached and stopped near us at the

watering hole. The men went to meet it, and it was agreed that we would bivouac the caravans in the same place that night, and, the next morning, each would go on their separate way.

That evening, everyone circled around the blazing flames, and I sat in the circle of women that was closest to the circle where the caravan leaders sat. There, I tried to listen to what they were saying. But, with the clamor of the great gathering, and with the talk of the women, I couldn't follow what they were saying, and could only pick out a few words. Then suddenly, I heard the phrase *caravan of slaves,* although I couldn't tell exactly what they were saying. I couldn't wait, and I went up to the leader of the other caravan.

"Excuse me, Sir, but were you talking about a caravan of slaves?"

He turned to me with an astonished look, surprised by my sudden appearance.

"Yes, a week ago we met with a slave caravan that was headed to Eden."

"Eden in Yemen?"

He laughed. "I don't know of any other Eden except that one," he said pointing toward the heavens, and I ignored his gesture and waited until he'd finished laughing.

"Did you hear about another caravan heading from Morocco to Egypt about two weeks ago?" I asked.

"I think it's the same caravan," he said. "The leader of the caravan told me he'd gotten sick during the journey, and his recovery delayed them. It was about ten days before they continued."

"And you said Eden, Sir?" I asked him urgently.

"That's what I said. A merchant told him that the price of slaves was higher in Eden than in Egypt, and so he decided to change course. I'd say that, about now, he'd be close to reaching Abyssinia."

"Abyssinia!" I shouted and began to weep. "Dear God! And did you see, on this caravan, a man and his daughter? They were captured after they were shipwrecked at sea. The man's name is Ahmed al-Maghribi and his daughter is Najma, and she wears a necklace like this, and on her neck there's a birthmark that looks like a berry…" Choked by tears, I couldn't finish.

The man tried to calm me down, and he called out, "Boy! Bring some water!"

He waited until I'd drunk and my tears had quieted.

"Now tell me your story in a calm way, so I might understand it."

So I told him about the ship, *Conqueror of the Sea* and how I knew that some of the survivors had been captured and sold as slaves, and that I had joined this caravan in order to follow the slave caravan and find my husband and daughter.

Everyone was silent.

"There is no power nor strength except in God," the man said, slapping one hand against the other.

"By God, please tell me, did you see a girl of about five years old with her father, who's named Ahmed?"

"I saw a number of men, women, and children, but I didn't pay much attention to them. I don't look closely at slaves. I'm sorry, I didn't mean…"

And he shook his head, embarrassed.

"You saw men and children," I insisted. "Please try to remember—a girl and her father."

"Forgive me, but I'm not sure. You know, in the caravans, free people don't mix with the sl…"

"Slaves, with the slaves," I finished. "Are you sure the caravan's been diverted to Eden? That we're talking about the same caravan that was headed to Egypt? He didn't tell you that part of the caravan had continued on to Egypt?"

"That's what I understood from him—the head of the caravan. He said slaves fetch a higher price in Eden, and that he'd sell the slaves and buy spices and incense."

"And how many days has it been since you saw that caravan?" I asked.

"Eight days exactly, and if everything's going well, the caravan will be nearing Abyssinia. The head of the caravan said something about buying slaves from there before sailing for Eden."

"Abyssinia, Abyssinia… Is there anyone here headed for Abyssinia?" I asked the leader of our caravan.

"No, this is a caravan of pilgrims, and most of them will continue on to the Arabian Peninsula."

"Are there any caravans that go from here to Abyssinia?"

"Not many—maybe one every few months."

"How can I reach them in Abyssinia before they set off for Yemen? Please, Sir, please help me find my husband and daughter."

He looked at me sadly.

"I'd very much like to help you, as your story moved me. But I don't know how I could, unless…"

He looked at the leader of the other caravan, who said nothing.

"Unless you wish to go with the pilgrims to the Arabian Peninsula. From there, you could ride with a caravan to Yemen."

"But that will take such a long time! Maybe it will be too late—please think, is there any other way?"

The leader of the caravan looked around, searching the other men's faces for a solution. "I want to help you. But what I've proposed is the only way."

Then silence fell, with some looking at the fire and some looking at me with sorrow and compassion, when suddenly a man I hadn't noticed before spoke.

"I will take the lady to Abyssinia."

A hum ran through the assembled group, and he directed his words to me.

"Excuse me, my lady, but did you say that your husband is Ahmed al-Maghribi from Kahraman Island?"

"Yes, yes." A glimmer of hope appeared before me. "Did you know my husband?"

"A man both noble and brave. He saved my life, and I still owe him a debt. I will do anything to pay back that gentleman."

The caravan leader interrupted.

"This is very touching, but I cannot allow her to leave the caravan in the company of a stranger. Every traveler in this caravan is my responsibility until reach Egypt."

"I am Zein al-Deen al-Ghafiqi of Kairouan," the man said angrily, "and I won't stand for this!"

"Yes, I know you. Who doesn't know the greatest merchant of Kairouan? But I cannot allow her to go. There are great dangers in this vast desert that two people cannot face alone. No, this is a venture with unforeseeable consequences."

"And who told you that we would be traveling alone?" asked Zein al-Deen, emphasizing every word. Then he stood and addressed the men loudly. "I will pay five hundred dirhams to each one of you who accompanies us to Abyssinia."

One man stood. "I'll come with you."

Another said, "Five hundred dirhams and a new coat."

"Five hundred dirhams and a new coat," said Zein al-Deen.

So another said, "Six hundred dirhams."

"Six hundred dirhams for every man," Zein al-Deen announced.

In the end, six men agreed to come with us.

"This is madness, Zein al-Deen," said the leader of the caravan. "There are still many dangers! It's an enormous desert, and you'll lose your way. And if you don't get lost, the bandits will kill you."

"My Abyssinian servant knows the desert well," Zein al-Deen said. "And he will be our guide."

"Please, Sir, allow him to take me to my husband and daughter," I pleaded. "I am willing to accept all these hardships and risks."

Our leader looked at the leader of the other caravan, who raised his hands to the heavens as though handing the decision over to God.

"Fine," our leader said. "But let everyone witness that I did not want to allow this woman to leave the caravan, and if anything happens to her, I am innocent of her blood."

12

GHOSTS FROM THE PAST

The next day at dawn, we parted ways with the caravan and headed south toward Sudan. We traveled much faster than the caravan, as there were few of us, and we traveled without women and children. I had become accustomed to riding camels and rode well, and whenever Mr. Zein al-Deen suggested that we rest, I would ask to continue, saying I wasn't tired.

Along the way, Zein al-Deen told me how my husband had saved his life.

He had been traveling to Genoa for trade and had met my husband, Ahmed, on the ship, which was hit by a great storm that almost capsized it. Zein al-Dein was thrown out onto the sea, and was sure he would die, but suddenly, he felt two hands gripping him and pulling him out of the water. Ahmed had seen him fall and had tied a rope around himself, then leapt into the water, risking his life to save him.

"But your husband saved my life twice," Zein al-Deen told me. "I also lost all my merchandise to the waters of the sea on that fateful voyage—I had put all my money into spices and lost it all. I returned to my country bankrupt, without knowing what to do. I came to the brink of despair and even thought of killing myself to rid myself of this bitter life. Then suddenly, like an angel from heaven, a messenger came bearing golden dinars, and he presented it to me saying it was from Ahmed al-Maghribi as a token of friendship so that I could start my business once again. He said he wasn't waiting for me to pay him back, but that this was a gift. And so, your husband has saved me from death twice." Then he added, laughing, "After that incident, I never traveled the seas again."

Our small caravan forged ahead, and Zein al-Deen was a good companion. His conversation was entertaining, and it helped restore my hope. He didn't burden me when he saw me sad or lonely. But, if my period of grief went on too long, he would say, "We'll find them, God willing. It's just a little farther now, we'll find them and you'll be together again." Then he would laugh. "And I'll be rid of the weight of this debt."

I would have liked it if we had ridden even faster, if we could have made the camels fly! I hurried the hours and hurried the camels, and finally, after crossing through Sudan and Abyssinia, we arrived in Djibouti. It seemed like the trip from Abyssinia to the Red Sea was longer than the entire distance we had traveled so far—but at last we arrived.

Zein al-Deen refused to let me come with him to the port to ask about slave caravans headed for Yemen, and I waited at the khan until, after a while, he returned to say that a ship loaded with slaves had left for Eden three days earlier. I asked him to find me a berth on the first ship headed there.

The next day, I bade him farewell.

"Thank you, Zein al-Deen, for your gallantry, generosity, and assistance. I will never forget this favor," I told him. Then I added, laughing, "Let everyone witness that I am freeing you from the debt you owe my husband, so you can return to your country free of it, and I will owe you all of my life."

He laughed.

"What's all this about debts?" he replied. "Your debt, my

164

debt. Thank God you're safe, and I hope you find your husband and daughter, and return to your homeland in peace. Better go now, the ship will be leaving soon."

And he stayed on the beach, waving, until we had gone far out to sea.

Later that day, we arrived on the shore of Eden, and as soon as I stepped off the ship, I began to ask about the ship of slaves but found no answer. A man, who was standing on the shore waiting for his goods to be loaded onto a ship, heard me asking about a slave ship that had arrived recently to Eden. He pointed me toward a khan frequented by merchants—someone there might have heard about the ship.

I went to the khan, took a room, and asked the owner about the traders. He pointed to a wealthy-looking man who stood with his back to me, talking to someone.

"That is the merchant, Abdullah," the innkeeper said. "He's well-traveled and knows all the merchants who pass through here."

So I approached the man.

"Excuse me, Sir, may I ask you a question?"

He turned to me, and when I saw his face, I gasped.

"Anfara! It's impossible—it can't be!"

"No one's called me that for years," the man said, surprised. "Do you know me?"

"Anfara," I said to him. "It's me!"

He continued to stare at me in great surprise.

"My name's Abdullah. May I help you, Sayyidati?" Then he added quietly, "How do you know my other name? Nobody knows it here except…"

I remembered that I was now a woman, and not Ajeeb the pirate, so how could he know me?

"Might we speak in private?" I asked him.

He excused himself from the conversation with the other man and led me to a corner where there were seats.

"Please sit down. I'm at your disposal, but I think you may want someone else."

"I want Anfara, who was first mate to the pirate Alaa al-Deen on the ship *The Black Angel*, who became its commander after the death of Alaa al-Deen, may God have mercy on his soul."

He looked around, careful that no one should hear us.

"How do you know all this? Were you close to the Captain Alaa al-Deen?"

I couldn't stop myself from smiling.

"I'm Ajeeb!"

"Excuse me?" he said, shocked.

"Okay," I said, "I'll start at the beginning. And please, don't interrupt. My name is Qamar, and I dressed in men's clothing to join your ship. But, let me start from the beginning."

And so, I told him about my home village in Palestine and the story of the curse, and how my mother solved the mystery and became a saint. I told him how my parents died and I left the village to live with my sister Shams and her husband and children, and about Um Najmuddin in Jerusalem. Then I told him about the caravan and the bandits and how I was sold into slavery. I explained about Noor al-Huda and the conspiracy against her, and how I went to Morocco and studied with the scholar, but then had to leave because I was a woman, and how I put on men's clothing to get on board the pirate ship, the *Black Angel*. And how I left when Alaa al-Deen died.

"Now I understand!" he said when I finished this part of my story. "Yes, now I get it. There were always things about your looks and actions I couldn't understand. But go on, go on, your story's interesting."

So I told him how, after Alaa al-Deen's death, I quit being a pirate and how I opened a bookshop with the gold he gave me.

"Do you remember how you gave me two bags full of gold pieces?"

"I remember, I remember… And I see you've done well. But go on."

Then I told him about my marriage to Ahmed, and about Najma, and about the happiness that had come to me at last. And then I told him how the ship sank, and there I began to cry.

He asked the khan's servant to bring us water and a hot honey drink, and I did my best to calm myself.

"Are you feeling better?" Anfara asked, with concern.

I nodded, and he looked at me, encouraging me to go on. So I finished my tale, about how I'd been thrown overboard in the storm and some fishermen on one of the Spanish islands had managed to save me after finding me nearly dead on a piece of wood. How I went to Tangier, and the story of the caravan to Egypt, and Zein al-Deen, who'd helped me get to Eden.

He sat there in silence, clearly troubled by all these unfortunate events. So, I waited for a little while, then I said laughing, "But it was a surprise to see you, and to learn that you've become a great merchant."

"After Alaa al-Deen died, we kept up the pirate life for a while. But then I decided to leave, to lead a decent life and take myself a wife."

"That's wonderful," I said. "Do you have children?"

"Yes. We have Alaa al-Deen and Heba, and my wife is pregnant."

"That is great news! And what happened to the rest of our friends from the *Black Angel*?"

"Monkey—remember him?"

"Of course," I said.

"He went to stay with his sick mother in their village, and I haven't heard from him since. Cabbage the cook died several months after you left, and his son works with me in trade. Abdoun and two others decided to go on with the pirate life, and the others scattered, as such is life."

"Yes, such is life."

He gave me a serious look.

"And now, Sayyidati…Qamar—or should I call you Ajeeb?"

"If you are now known as Abdullah, then I should be called Qamar."

"Well, Qamar, then not only do I promise, but I swear on my life, which you once saved, that I won't spare any effort or wealth to find your husband and daughter. Now rest, and I'll be back after I've asked some of the merchants about this slave ship."

That same evening he returned.

"I found you the merchant who bought the slaves. He is well-known around here. People call him Al-Jazzar, "the butcher," because he's very brutal and vicious. So we need to be very careful when we talk to him.

I almost flew from joy—I was going to find Ahmed and Najma this very night!

Only later, on the way to the merchant's house, did his words sink in. Al-Jazzar, the name itself—"terrified me. All they way to the slaver's house, memories came back to me. The horrible fearful bandit leader in the desert ,being driven into the streets of Cairo in chains, the exhaustion, the humiliation, the fear of an unknown future. *Please God, help me save my loved ones from such a fate.*

We arrived at the home of this merchant, Al-Jazzar. He treated us coldly. Anfara told him about me, and about the shipwreck, and about my long journey in search of my husband

and daughter. He also offered him a large sum of money, in compensation, if we found Ahmed and Najma among his slaves.

As Al-Jazzar listened, his features showed no emotion. After Anfara had finished, I told him, "My husband is in mid-forties," and I described him in detail. "And my daughter's around five, and her name is Najma, and she wears a necklace like this, and on the left side of her neck there's a birthmark in the shape of a berry. Please, take me to them."

"I purchased all the slaves who arrived from Tangier and Abyssinia, and I have not yet sold them. But I don't remember a man or a girl of those descriptions—"

"It's not possible!" I cried out. "My husband and daughter must be with them, please take me to them now."

Displeased, the merchant looked impatiently at Anfara, who said, "Get hold of yourself, Qamar. We'll go to them."

"Take me to them now," I told them.

And then I stood, and the two men stood as well.

"Alright," Al-Jazzar said. "Let's go. But don't get your hopes up. Your husband and daughter may have drowned."

"No, it's not possible. They're here."

We went to the back of the house, where we headed down an alleyway. When we reached a door, the merchant took out a bunch of keys and opened it slowly.

"Please, faster," I urged him.

I imagined Najma running to me and wrapping me in her two little arms, and Ahmed with his broad smile, saying, "I knew you'd come."

Carrying a lamp, Al-Jazzar entered before us. Then he barked out to the huddled people, "Get up and stand by the wall."

I went in behind him, and he passed the lamp in front of the face of each of these unfortunate slaves—sad face after sad face, each disfigured by grief—crying children, and mothers clutching their babies to their breasts. I pitied them so, and the memory of how I'd been in a place like this flooded over me.

"That's all of them," Al-Jazzar said.

I didn't see Ahmed or Najma's face in this miserable gathering, but I refused to believe it.

"Are there other rooms?"

"That's it, that's the lot.

I didn't hear the rest of his words, because everything went dark. When I awoke, I opened my eyes to discover Anfara's worried face gazing at me, and I looked around and found myself resting on a comfortable bed, in a strange room.

"Thank God you're okay, we were worried about you," he said.

"Where am I?"

"At the house of my good friend, Jassem, and his wife. He lives close to the slaver's house. You passed out, and I carried you here."

I sat up in bed, feeling like I might suffocate.

"I couldn't find them, Anfara. Ahmed and Najma…I couldn't find them!"

"I know, I know," he replied anxiously. "Right now, I want you to get better. Then we'll think about what to do."

"I couldn't find them! I couldn't find them, Anfara!"

"Rest now, and don't think about anything except getting better." He stood up. "I'm going to bring you some food."

"I don't want food, I don't want to eat."

But despite my protests, he left and returned after a short while with Jassem and a woman about Um Najmuddin's age, who was carrying a tray of food.

Jassem said, "This is my wife, Um Saad."

The woman stepped forward and put the tray on a table beside me, then sat on the edge of the bed.

"Thank God you're alright, daughter. Won't you eat something?"

"Thank you, but I don't want to eat."

"I understand your situation, and the grief you have suffered, but you have to eat something."

"I'm not hungry."

Um Saad looked over at her husband, who also seemed concerned.

"Well, rest a little, you might be hungry later. For now, we'll leave you to rest." The merchant gestured for his wife to leave. Before she did, she gave my hand a gentle pat, and then her husband followed.

Anfara remained beside me.

"Rest now, Qamar. I'll come back to see you in the morning."

Rest! How could I rest? I couldn't even cry! I lay on my back, staring at the ceiling, feeling nothing, as though my body had been emptied of everything, down to my soul, and all I had left was this unfeeling shell. I didn't notice the passage of time, or the darkness that had begun to overtake the room.

I heard a knock at the door, saw a lamplight creeping, and heard the sound of footsteps, but I didn't move or turn toward the lamp to find out who had come in. I just looked at the dim ceiling, which had begun to dance with the shadows thrown by the lamp. I heard Um Saad's voice saying, "Qamar, are you asleep, my girl?" But I didn't answer. I just kept staring at the ceiling, as if my eyes were connected to it by an invisible thread. Um Saad came up to the bed, and I felt her breath on my face as she examined me.

"Qamar? Qamar, do you hear me? Answer me!"

I didn't move, and she sat beside me and took my hand.

"My God," she said in a frightened voice. "Your hand is as cold as ice!"

I didn't answer—not because I didn't want to, but because I couldn't, and my gaze still clung to the ceiling, as if something prevented me from moving or speaking. I was trapped in a dark place, unable to pull myself out of it. She gave my shoulder a rough shake, and then I felt a strong slap against my cheek. The slap moved my head toward her, and I looked at her.

"What happened to you?" she asked. "You're frightening me. Please say something."

I didn't answer. I couldn't force my tongue to move, or my throat to push out the words. It was as if something had damaged my brain, and I no longer had the power to move my body, and even my thoughts...nothing. My eyes were drawn back to the ceiling.

Um Saad left the room, panicked, and returned with her husband, who I heard say, "Qamar, are you alright? Answer me. Say something, anything!"

I felt him there for a long time before he went out with his wife, and they returned with Anfara, who stood beside the bed.

"Qamar, what's going on? Come on, say something," Anfara pleaded. "This isn't right, Qamar, please!" Then he struck one hand against the other. "There's no power nor strength except in God—it's better if we bring a doctor."

And the three of them left the room.

When they came back, I heard a new voice say, "*Al salaam alaikum,*" and I felt him sit at the edge of the bed and take my hand. Then he put a hand to my eye, trying to open it, and he put his face close to mine, breathing on me, so that all I saw of his face were two reddened eyes, as if he had just now been woken. Then, he sat back and took my hand in his.

"Can you hear me? I'm Dr. Abdel-Azim. Do you feel anything, my dear? Look at me and tell me what you feel."

But even though I could hear him, I couldn't will my body

to do anything. It was as though my body were acting on its own and my soul was somewhere else. The doctor looked at me for a while, and took my pulse.

"Has she eaten anything?" he asked.

"Not since yesterday," the woman said. "This is how she's been since morning, staring at the ceiling, not moving, not answering."

The doctor stood up.

"This woman has suffered a powerful shock."

"Yes, she lost her husband and her daughter," Anfara said. "But is there a cure for her condition? We're worried about her."

"I'm afraid that, in such a situation, there is no specific treatment, as each individual defends themself against a strong shock in a different way. There's no medicine that can be taken— only some herbs to stimulate the nerves. Give her plenty of water, milk, juices, and remain nearby. The rest is in God's hands."

"But will she be like this for long?" Anfara asked.

"It's hard to say—days, weeks. God is merciful to his creations."

I heard him leave and felt Anfara come sit beside me and take my hand.

"There is no power nor strength except in God," he said in a low voice. "Don't you believe in God, Qamar?"

He was silent for a while.

"You're the only one who can cure yourself, Qamar. Come on, pull yourself out of this and come back to us."

But I kept staring at the ceiling.

"Try to give her some water," he said to Um Saad, "and I'll come back to check on her in the morning."

And they all went out.

Um Saad returned and sat beside me. Gently, she lifted my head in her left hand and put a glass of water to my lips, saying, "Drink a little, just one sip. Come on, my child, come on, you're breaking my heart." When I didn't respond, she set my head down, parted my lips with her fingers, and started to dribble the water into my mouth. I began to choke and had to swallow, and she said, with satisfaction, "That's better. It will give you a bit of strength."

She moved away from the bed, and I heard her whisper to her husband, who I hadn't noticed was in the room. "She drank a bit of water, thank God," she said. And they left.

I don't know how many days I remained like that, with Um Saad forcing me to take a little water or some juice or an herbal infusion. She knew the ruse: a dribble into my mouth would force me to either choke or swallow. Once, she tried to give me some water on a spoon, but that didn't work, and she went back to pouring water and other drinks into my mouth. I could feel when Anfara came, several times a day, to ask Um Saad about me, and she'd always answer, "Nothing new, still in the same condition," and I could hear them talking, wondering when this would come to an end, and then Anfara would leave.

I could always feel Um Saad's presence in the room, even when she wasn't offering me water or drinks, sitting beside me in silence, or sometimes talking about many things—herself, her husband, her children, the city of Eden, the weather, the sea, the garden. It was as though, with her continuous flow of talk, she was trying to draw me out of my lost state.

I could hear her, but I couldn't respond or answer her words. Yet, while she got no reaction from me, she went on talking as she fed me, washed me, or combed my hair. One day, Um Saad sat beside me, chattering away as usual.

"Look, what a lovely morning. Can you hear the sound of the birds singing? The flowers have bloomed in the garden. I'll have to bring some of them into your room."

Then she said, "Time for a bath," and began to take off my clothes and wipe my body with a damp, perfumed cloth. As she gently put my clothes back on, she spoke to me.

"The necklace you wear is very beautiful. Your husband gave it to you right before your journey, isn't that right? Abdullah told me about it. He said your husband had two of them made, one for you and the other for your daughter Najmat al-Sabah. Oh, he must have loved you so much. May God have mercy…"

I looked at her, and tears began to fall from my eyes, and she clutched me to her chest and said, "Cry, my child. Cry."

With a voice that wasn't my own, I said, "They're gone!"

I began to weep bitter and painful tears, the tears of the bereft. I began to scream with all the power and breath that remained in my lungs, and I turned away from her and wrenched at my hair as I screamed and called out. And after I had exhausted myself with screaming, I went back to weeping—such weeping that I don't know how my frail body found the strength.

I don't know how long I went on crying—for a time I put my head on Um Saad's shoulder, and for a time I pulled away, yanking my hair and slapping my face. Then the world darkened again.

When I awoke, Um Saad was still at my side, and I found Anfara standing near the bed, and Jassem close beside him. Anfara grinned when I opened my eyes.

"That's better. Thank God you're back. You really gave us a fright when you weren't moving, and you've got so thin! What do you say to some food?"

"I've lost them." I said to him, weakly.

"No," he said, trying to give me courage. "You don't know that for sure. Maybe they were saved. Maybe you'll still find them. Trust in God."

175

"What will I do now? Tell me, what will I do?"

"The first thing you need to do is to get your health back," he said, trying to put some cheer in his voice. "You're wasting away, and you can't think in such a condition. Drink this," he added, handing me a bowl of soup that had been on the table beside me.

"I have no desire to eat."

"You have to eat something," he said firmly. "For me, and for this good lady who sat beside you and didn't leave you for even one moment. Come on, please."

I drank two or three spoonfuls of soup and returned the bowl to him.

"Yes," he said. "That's better."

"What will I do now?" I asked again.

"How about a walk with me in the garden?" Um Saad offered. "The weather is lovely, and you haven't been out of this room for three weeks. Your body needs fresh air, come on."

She took hold of my hand to help me onto my feet.

And Jassem said, "Abdullah and I will have coffee or honey drink with you in the garden."

I tried to stand, but my legs were too weak, and I stumbled. Um Saad reached out a hand and helped me to stand, and she kept on supporting me until we reached the garden.

I sat on one of the chairs, and she stretched a wool cloth over my knees so that I wouldn't catch a chill. The light was so intense that I had to close my eyes for a while, until they adjusted to it. Um Saad, Jassem, and Anfara sat around me in silence. We listened to the sounds of the birds and the trees, and for a long time no one said anything, as if they were afraid that any word might set off my tears, or perhaps they just wanted to give me a chance to slowly get used to the light and sounds around me.

But I wasn't paying any attention to my surroundings; I was lost in the wilderness of my thoughts. *They couldn't have drowned, I can't accept it, but…oh God, please don't let them be taken as slaves. Being chained in the belly of a ship, packed like starving creatures, suffocating from lack of air and the smell of bodies and sweat and excrement. No, no one should ever be stolen from their homes, or have to see their loved ones taken away and sold. Oh, please God let them be safe, or let them be dead but not suffer this fate.*

Anfara noticed the silent tears streaming down my cheeks, and he gave me an affectionate look but said nothing, leaving me to deal with my demons in peace. When the silence had stretched out for a while, he began to talk to Jassem about trade and upcoming travels, as if he were diverting attention away from me.

"I heard you were going to India. When's that?" asked Jassem.

"Perhaps in the next two months," said Anfara. "I'm still collecting and preparing the merchandise: gum Arabic, incense from Socotra Island, coffee, dates, daggers and swords. What do you think about joining me?"

"No, no, I'm too old now to go on such a journey. Even to sit in the shop and follow the dealings there exhausts me. So how could I travel? No, excuse me from this honor, although if you need a business partner, then that's something I can do."

"What are you talking about, man?" Anfara said, joking. "You're still a young man, capable of marrying three girls of twenty at the same time. Isn't that so, Um Saad?"

Um Saad laughed. "If that's the case, then he should travel."

Everyone laughed, and then they looked at me. But I couldn't join in their fun. I was still trapped in my thoughts. Their voices were so distant, as they were if coming from a world far away.

For another month I stayed in the home of Jassem and Um Saad, and in truth they were good and gentle with me. I would spend hours crying or wandering around the garden, and Um Saad would keep me under her watchful eye. It wasn't until she saw me start to cry that she would hurry to my side, trying to comfort me.

I had no desire for anything, even to think. The days were tasteless, each hour and day like another. Then sadness would come over me every time that horrifying image of my loved ones being enslaved came to mind. And my heart would sink, and I'd feel a pain crushing my body. *What should I do? Where do I look for them? No sign of them in Tangier, and none in Eden! Where are they?*

I refused to believe, or let myself be persuaded, that they had drowned, nor could I accept that they had been taken as slaves. When I reached this point in my thoughts, I went back to feeling that I was alone and drowning, and that there was no one to help me find an answer, nor even a thread of hope to which I could cling. Those were the harshest, cruelest days of my life.

Finally came the day that Anfara asked the question I had been hesitant to even to think about.

"What do you mean to do? Will you go back to Tangier?"

"There's nothing left for me there."

"So will you go back to Palestine?" he asked.

"I don't know!"

In truth, this was how I felt about everything. My desires had died, and I no longer wanted anything. As I began to convince myself that I had lost them forever, life no longer had value or meaning—what was the meaning of a life without those I loved? How could life have flavor when everything I loved was gone? I wouldn't be able to stay here, and I had to go somewhere, it didn't matter where. So I said, "I think I will return to Palestine, since there is nothing for me elsewhere."

"Let this be the will of God, and..."

Anfara was silent.

"Would you...?" he asked, hesitantly. But then he didn't finish his question, and I didn't urge him to.

My health improved a little, thanks to Um Saad's perseverance, and I began to feel strong enough to travel back to my country. That evening, I told her.

"I've decided to go back to Palestine."

Um Saad gasped and pressed a hand to her mouth.

"So fast? Stay a little, until you're better."

"I think I'm well enough for the journey."

"I don't know what it will be like without you," she said. "I've gotten so used to you! The house will be so gloomy. Stay a bit."

"I don't know how to thank you for all you've done for me these months, for your care and generosity. But it's time for me to leave and go back to my country."

Um Saad tried to convince me to change my mind, or to prolong my time with her. But when Anfara came to visit that evening, I asked him to find me a place in a caravan bound for Palestine.

"Are you sure you want to go back there?" he asked.

"Where else should I go?" I asked, bitterly. "There's nothing for me anywhere else. I'll go back to my village and stay there until I die."

"You talk like you're a hundred years old!" he said. "You're what—thirty-three, thirty-four?

I tried to force a smile.

"Alright, thirty-eight?"

I took a breath, and nodded.

"You're still too young to think this way!"

"My life is over, can't you see that? I don't want anything from this world. This will be the last time I travel, to go back to my country. And then I don't want anything else. I'm tired, and what I've lost can't be replaced, not anywhere."

"Well, have it your way. If you want to bury yourself alive in that lonely village, it's your own business."

"Yes," I replied angrily. "It's my business, and that's what I want to do."

"I'll ask around tomorrow about caravans headed to Palestine," he said.

He came back the next day to say there was a caravan headed to Palestine in two weeks, and that he had reserved me a place in it.

Two weeks passed, and the time came for me to leave. I had begun to pack up my clothes when Anfara came in.

"The caravan's leaving tomorrow morning, and the travelers will meet at a khan in the center of the city. I'll come before you leave to bid farewell." He hesitated a moment, then he said, "Are you still determined to travel back to your homeland? You won't change your mind?"

"What else would I do?" I asked. "I've lost everything!"

"But you haven't lost yourself. What about…?"

"What about what?"

He spoke quickly, as if afraid his words might betray him.

"What about traveling to India? My ship's traveling there in two weeks. And there's nothing in Palestine to make you rush back, I mean…you'll see a new county and then you'll go home. What about that?"

"That's very kind of you, my friend, but I can't. I don't want to travel, or to learn about new countries."

"Where's the pirate Ajeeb, who was always thirsting for

something new? Come on, he must be in there somewhere."

"Ajeeb died," I said bitterly. "And before you stands the ruins of Qamar."

"I don't think so," he said. "You're a person who's brave and strong, and who can overcome anything."

"Those days have come and gone. All my courage has been destroyed."

"That's not true. You still long to see the world. Those who do can never stop wanting to see more."

"I've seen enough to stop."

His tone changed. "But I need you."

"You need *me*?" I said. "Me?"

"It's a big ship with a lot of sailors and merchants and passengers. We need a doctor with us at all times—this isn't a pirate ship...And I don't know of one better than you. Come on, say yes."

"Thanks for the flattery. But I don't think I can ride the seas anymore."

"Don't answer now. You have until tomorrow, so take your time and I'll accept whatever you decide. But please, just take your time thinking about it."

"Alright. You have my word."

"Don't you feel a nostalgia for the good old days?" he added, as though he were holding the last straw.

"We aren't pirates, Anfara. Not anymore."

"I don't mean piracy. I mean traveling, journeying, adventuring—discovering new things."

I smiled bitterly.

"It must be inside you somewhere. Look for it."

"I will."

As I'd promised him, I thought about it. But I couldn't rediscover my sense of adventure. I felt as if all of my emotions had died, that I was too old and tired, and I wanted a place where I could bury myself and my grief. My village was the perfect place. There, I could live out the rest of my days with no taste for the savor of life. There was nothing that could lessen my immense sadness, and travel can't amuse the bereaved. If I had been offered something like this trip to India years ago—before I found happiness and peace with Ahmed and Najma—I would have jumped with joy and gone without hesitation. But now…

I couldn't sleep that night.

The next day, Anfara arrived.

"So, have you decided? Have we got ourselves a doctor?"

"The truth is, I stayed up all night thinking that tomorrow the caravan will go to my country, and maybe I'd better go with it. Every adventure has only brought me more pain and sadness. I no longer have the energy for it."

"As you like," he said, disappointed. "But that means I have to go find myself a doctor."

"Good luck. I'm sure you'll find a brilliant one."

"Yes, yes."

He had a sorrowful look.

"Then I'll be here early tomorrow to take you to the caravan and see you off. Who knows when we might meet again?"

My parting with Um Saad was sad, just as the parting with Um Najmuddin had been years before. It was hard to take leave of this woman who had embraced me with her tenderness, love, and care. The merchant Jassem instructed a servant to carry my bags, and I bid him farewell and walked with Anfara in silence toward the khan where the passengers would meet.

As we approached the khan, I stopped and looked at the camels, and the travelers' bags carefully packed on top of them, and the crowds of travelers.

I thought for a moment.

Then I told the servant who was carrying my bags, "Please take them to the merchant Abdullah's ship."

I turned to Anfara, whose face had lit up with a big smile.

"I didn't ask you the name of the ship."

He laughed joyfully and turned to the servant.

"Please take the doctor's bags to *The Jewel*.

4

13

THE SEA AGAIN

I stood at the railing of *The Jewel*, waving to Jassem and Um Saad, and wiping my tears. When they'd learned I would travel with Abdullah to India, they had welcomed the idea. All the previous week, I had tried to convince myself this was the right decision. I sent a letter for my sister Shams with the caravan to Palestine, telling her about everything that had happened. As the ship moved away from the shore, Um Saad still stood there waving with her handkerchief. Then the port disappeared, and we were at sea.

That's when whispery emotions swept over me, and memories rushed back, of Najma running and jumping on board the ship, which made a painful, thorny lump in my throat. Then, I felt the touch of a gentle hand and heard a familiar voice.

"Welcome Ajeeb, Madam."

I turned to find Hamid, the son of Cabbage, the pirate cook, standing beside me. Laughing joyfully, he gave me a wink with his good eye; the other was covered with the leather patch I'd made for him after he'd lost that eye in a battle on board the ship. We greeted each other warmly. He said he left piracy behind when they sold the *Black Angel* to a novice, and he continued to work with Anfara in trade and was with him still.

Then he said, "Anfara told me your story—it's a terrible shame."

But when he saw tears beginning to gather in my eyes, he quickly changed tack, speaking cheerfully.

"Now that you're here, and we're back together again, what do you think? Shall we attack a ship on our way?"

I laughed through my tears. "Aren't you tired of that business?"

"You know, I'm a trader now. But at times I still get the itch to fight in a battle. The lives of respectable men are boring, bah! I'd give anything for a good battle."

"Was fighting ever good? I hated being forced to carry a sword, and I never loved the violence."

"Well, now that I know you're a woman, I understand. You know, when we pass another ship, I say to Anfara, 'That would make a precious catch—what do you think?'"

"And what does Anfara say?"

"He says, 'Those days are done and gone.'"

The days on *The Jewel* passed quietly, and I sat for hours watching the sea, meditating on my life, giving vent to my grief, and weeping over the only happiness I'd ever known. Then one day, while I was dozing in the comfortable seat Anfara had brought just for me, I felt a hand tug at my sleeve. It was a dark-skinned girl of about ten years old, looking at me shyly.

"Are you really a doctor?" she asked.

"Not exactly. But how did you know?"

"Captain Abdullah sent me to you."

"And how can I help you, little one?"

"My mother is very sick," she said. "Can you help her?"

"Of course. Take me to her."

And she took hold of my hand and led me to the stairs. When I felt her small hand in mine, I remembered Najma's slender hand tightening around mine whenever she saw something that caught her eye.

I knocked on the door and stepped inside. Her mother was dark-skinned like her and wearing a bright-colored Indian sari. She lay on the bed with a hand on her forehead. The little one spoke fluent Arabic.

"Mother," she said. "I brought you a doctor."

The woman sat up slowly in bed and gave a weak smile.

"How are you?" I asked. "What's troubling you?"

"I have pain all over my body," she said in unsteady Arabic. "And it feels like flames are coming out of my head."

I put my hand to her forehead and felt that her temperature was very high.

"It's a fever, but don't worry. I'll bring you some herbs." I had bought large amounts of herbs in Eden to have when necessary. "Don't worry, I'll be back shortly," I told her.

I took out some herbs, prepared them in the ship's kitchen, and gave them to the woman. Some were to help her sleep.

"Rest now, and I'll come back to check on you."

I went out, and the little girl followed.

"Can I help? Is there anything I can do to help her?"

I gave her a tender smile.

"No, we should leave her be. What do you think of taking a tour of the ship?"

She grabbed my hand, and we went aboveboard and wandered around the deck. I took her to the quarters of Captain Abdullah, who welcomed us and explained all about how to sail a ship. After we'd finished the tour, I returned to sit in my chair and the girl sat beside me.

"What's your name?" I asked her.

"Fatima," she said. "What's yours?"

"Qamar."

"That's a beautiful name."

Then she was silent for a while before she looked at me again.

"Is Captain Abdullah your husband?" she asked.

I was surprised.

"No, what makes you think that?"

"Don't you have a husband?"

Children—no taboos! All innocence.

"No," I said. "I had a husband, and a lovely daughter like you. But they're lost now, and I'm still looking for them."

"How did they get lost?"

"That's a long story. I'll tell you one day."

"I don't have a father. Mine died a year ago."

I felt this little one's need for kindness, having suffered loss as I had. I took both her hands in mine.

"Such is life. Sometimes we have to keep going without the people we love."

I was trying to ease her burden with these words, and I wished I were convinced by them myself. But I still felt unable to go on without Ahmed and Najma. She started to cry.

"Please don't," I told her, "because I'll cry too."

She leaned against my chest.

"My father was really nice. He gave me lots of presents. But after he died, my grandma made us leave the house, and I heard her tell my mom, 'Go back to the country where my son found you!'"

"Really!?"

"After my grandma kicked us out, my mother worked as a servant for some families. But in the end, she decided to go back to India and her people."

I pressed her more tightly against my chest and didn't know what to say except, "Let's go see your mother."

When we got back to their room, Rajna, Fatima's mother, was still lying down with her eyes closed. But when she noticed us come in, she opened her eyes and sat up in the bed.

"Keep resting," I said. "How do you feel?"

"Much better, thank you."

Then she reached out a hand toward her daughter, who took it gently and sat beside her.

"Fatima told me about what happened to you," I said. "How terrible! How can people be so cruel?"

"They can be even worse, my lady, believe me."

"I hope you reach your country safely and that your story has a happy ending," I said. "Now it's time for your second dose."

I poured out more of the herbs for her. Then I left her to rest.

By the time we reached India, Rajna had recovered, and in the days before we arrived, she'd managed to walk around with us on the deck. My relationship with her and her daughter had grown so much that Fatima didn't want to leave my side, and I loved her very much. I had already told Rajna my story and how I came to lose my loved ones. Grief brought us together— each of us found in the others a refuge from our sorrows, and we wept for what we'd lost and wiped each other's tears.

From the moment we reached Mumbai, the ship bustled with activity. Anfara came to find me.

"It's going to be a while before we finish unloading goods from the ship. Why don't you go with Rajna and Fatima to the khan? There's a carriage waiting. I'll meet with you later."

I didn't see Anfara until the next morning.

"Forgive me, it's taken me so long to unload the ship, and I still have much to do. I wanted to take you on a tour of the city."

"You finish your work, and I'll go into the city with Rajna and Fatima."

So all day, we toured the city, and I bought clothes for Fatima and Rajna, and some for myself. That evening, before Anfara arrived, Rajna asked, "What do you think about coming along to the village with me?"

"No," I said. "What would I do there? You will be reunited with your family. And I should stay with the ship in case Captain Abdullah needs me."

"And what will you do here in this city, alone? Come with us, and you'll get to know the countryside and be a companion to me and Fatima."

Fatima clung to me. "Please say yes. I can't stand to be away from you."

"You'll die of boredom here alone," Rajna said. "Come on, say yes."

Really, what will I do in this city alone? And I didn't come to India just to see one city! And I am not sure that Abdullah will need me, since all the passengers and sailors have departed the ship."

"Alright," I said, "I'll come with you. But I need to be back before the ship leaves for Eden."

Rajna brightened, and Fatima grabbed me with both hands and hugged me.

When Anfara came that evening, I told him about my decision.

"But…!" he said.

"But what? Are you afraid for me?"

"I wouldn't be afraid for you—even if you were surrounded by wild animals. But you'll be back before the ship sets out for Eden, won't you? A month from today— don't be late."

"A month from today, I'll be on board *The Jewel*."

"Alright. I'll find a guide and a guard, to be sure you're safe."

"Do we really need a guard?"

"Yes, you'll be going through forests, and there will be bandits and wild animals. I don't want anything to happen to you."

"Thank you, friend."

The next day, I was stunned to find an elephant standing in the lane by the port, surrounded by four heavily armed guards.

"Your carriage is ready, Sayyidati." Abdullah said, smiling.

"Where?" I asked.

He gestured toward the elephant.

"You're joking."

"In this country, elephant is the best way to travel. Don't worry, it will be fun."

"But it's an elephant."

Rajna, who was listening in on our exchange, laughed.

"Don't worry," she said. "They aren't any harder to ride than a camel."

I stepped down from the ship, and the elephant's keeper stood, holding one of its ears. Suddenly, the elephant lowered itself to the ground. On its back was a box, and a man gestured for me to get in, and to my surprise, I found that it was spacious inside and had comfortable seats. Rajna stepped up, and Fatima was amazed and excited, as she'd never seen anything like it before.

"And remember to be here on time," Abdullah reminded me. "Because there won't be favorable winds after that."

"Don't worry! I'll be here."

And so, we traveled through green fields, and even though the elephant was walking calmly, I was afraid that I would fall off. But as we went on, I began to feel more comfortable and was able to enjoy the landscape around me, and to see the people working in the fields—it truly was a beautiful country! We rested not far from them from time to time, but they kept working, indifferent to us.

Along the way, Rajna told me her story. She said she had many sisters and brothers, and that her father worked as a laborer for a maharaja. He earned little, even though his children worked alongside him, and there was barely enough to feed this army of mouths.

Rajna was the eldest of the girls, very beautiful, and by the age of fifteen, she was also working in the fields. One day, the Maharaja's son passed by. He was spoiled, entitled, and two years older than Rajna. He saw her and admired her beauty, and what the Maharaja's son wants, he gets. He ordered some of his guards to bring her to him, but she refused. The boy threatened that if Rajna didn't come to him, her father would lose his job. So, she decided to flee to Mumbai, a city on the sea, far from the Maharaja's son.

In the city, she worked as a housemaid, and one morning she was buying vegetables for her mistress when a speeding carriage passed and nearly crushed Rajna beneath its wheels. She fell to the ground and the vegetables in her basket were scattered. A handsome Arab man stepped down from the carriage and apologized, and, when he saw her beauty, he fell in love and asked where she lived. The next day, he came to her master's house and asked for her hand. He gave him a large sum of money and took her with him to a ship headed for Yemen, and there on the ship, they were married. Yet, when they arrived at his house in the Hijaz, on the Arabian Peninsula, his mother refused to accept their marriage. She screamed and pulled at her hair, saying, "You refuse all the respectable girls in this city, and bring home a maidservant from India! You shame me in front of everyone!"

This went on the whole time they were married. Even after Fatima was born and grew up, the grandmother remained the same and refused to visit her son's house.

Rajna was silent for a bit.

"I was happy with my husband. He was a good and generous man, but his mother…Then my husband fell ill. The medicines did nothing for him, and he died in my arms. His mother came even before we'd buried him, and she told me, 'There's nothing left for you in this country. Leave this house.' And you know the rest. I don't know if my family is still where I left them, or whether the Maharaja threw them out. I've heard nothing from them since I ran away."

She looked at me sadly.

"I'm afraid I was hasty in inviting you to come with me, because here you are on a journey without knowing what might come of it. I'm sorry."

"Whatever happens, I am with you," I said. "We'll face what comes together, and who knows—maybe your family is right where they were, waiting for your return!"

Fatima was sleeping in her lap, and Rajna was stroking her hair.

"Oh Lord, I hope."

Two days passed, and we rode between fields, eating under trees, and at night we slept beneath them, too. Then, on the third day, at nightfall, we approached the edge of a forest. We ate our food and wrapped ourselves in blankets to sleep, as the guards whispered among themselves.

I dozed a little, and then suddenly opened my eyes, as if awakened by a premonition. I looked around, and in the place of the two camps, there was silence and shadows. I couldn't see the guards, or the elephant's keeper, or even the elephant, which had still been chewing leaves when I fell asleep. I felt wretched, and I called out to the guards, but was answered with silence.

Rajna woke to my call, as did Fatima, who rubbed her eyes.

"What's wrong?" Rajna asked. "What happened?"

"The guards, the guide, the elephant. They've all disappeared!"

"And our things?"

"They stole everything!"

We were at the edge of the forest without our belongings, or food, or money, or shelter. Rajna began to scream and weep, and Fatima came up and wrapped her arms around her, and the two of them cried together. I stood in place, stunned. Our situation was precarious—we now had nothing. I should have cried, but I started to laugh, and tears fell as I laughed. Rajna and Fatima stopped crying and looked at me in surprise. I looked at them, clutching my sides from laughing so hard, and they were astonished, looking at me as though I'd been touched by a *jinn*, or a powerful demon.

"Why are you laughing?" Rajna asked. "This is very bad!"

But I couldn't answer her, and I had to sit down because I couldn't hold myself up. I said, my voice coming out in gasps, "They stole everything!"

"Yes," she said. "They stole everything, but it isn't funny. Have you gone mad?"

I started laughing again, and Rajna shook me with both hands. I pulled her hands off me and wiped the tears from my cheeks.

"Don't you find this situation funny?"

"I find it very sad, and I don't understand why you're laughing!"

I tried to stand up, and she reached out a hand to help me up.

"Every trip I've taken, something terrible has happened. It's as if it were written in the book of fate, that, at every step, I should face some perilous test. I was expecting a storm to hit the ship we were on. When nothing happened, I thought maybe my fate had changed. But something new was waiting for me—we were robbed by the ones who were meant to protect us! Isn't this a nice trick for fate to play on us? Don't you find that funny?"

"So far, I haven't found anything you said funny. Please come back to your senses so we can figure out what to do."

"Yes, yes, let's see what we should do."

I looked all around us, and it was dark.

"We won't be able to find our way through the forest now. I think we should stay here until morning. Let's try to start a fire."

We collected what we could of firewood and dry leaves, and spent a long time rubbing the wood together to get a spark. Finally, we got the fire going and sat around it. Fatima rested her head on her mother's thigh and fell asleep, and I told Rajna she should try to sleep while I kept guard. So she leaned back against a tree and closed her eyes. I remained watchful, no longer worried about thieves or bandits, but afraid that some animal would attack us, as there were many in India's jungles.

Ever since I'd left Tangier on the last caravan, I'd carried a small knife in my belt, in case of trouble, and now I took it out. I found a dry branch nearby and set it at my side, so I could strike anything that came near. I kept throwing wood on the fire so that predators wouldn't approach.

I tried to keep my eyes open and stay alert, but against my will they began to close. I tried to hold them wide open so I wouldn't fall asleep, but I couldn't keep at it, so I told myself, *I'll close my eyes just for a second so I'm more comfortable, but I'll stay awake.* But, as they say, sleep is a powerful master, and I dozed off where I was sitting.

I woke up with a jolt as Fatima suddenly started screaming and writhing. In a panic, I ran to her in time to see a poisonous snake flee—she'd been bitten in the leg by a viper! I had to do something, but for a moment I just stood there, paralyzed by fear and confusion, until Rajna shouted, "Do something, please, she'll die!"

I cut Fatima's leg with the dagger and pressed at the edges of the bite to push out the poison in the blood. Then I put my lips over the bite and began to suck the poison and spit it out. I tied my scarf around her leg, above the wound, and tightened the knot to prevent the poison from spreading to the rest of her body.

Then I took a burning coal out of the fire and said to Fatima, "This will hurt, are you ready?" She nodded, and I said to Rajna, "Hold her tight."

Her mother held her, and I put the blazing coal directly on the wound. Fatima screamed and fainted, and the wound oozed smoke and the smell of burning skin. When I was done treating her, Rajna and I wept at the sight of her little crumpled body in her mother's lap. Her mother rocked her gently.

"Perhaps it's best that she fainted," I said to Rajna. "She wouldn't have been able to bear all this pain. We'll try to head back to the last village we passed, with the first morning light."

We didn't sleep for the rest of the night, we were so worried about Fatima, who didn't stop whimpering and moaning. At dawn, Rajna picked up Fatima, and we began to hurry back toward the village. When Rajna tired, I carried Fatima, without stopping to rest. It seemed the road went on forever.

Finally, we came to a small house at the edge of a field, where a woman was drawing water from a well and pouring it into a brass jar. Rajna called out as we approached the woman, and she explained our situation while I carried Fatima and whispered in her ear that she shouldn't be afraid. "We've made it, now we'll get you some help. Don't be afraid, sweetheart."

The woman quickly opened the door and gestured for

us to go inside. I laid Fatima on a mattress on the floor in a modest room and asked for water, sprinkling several drops onto Fatima's lips. Then, I asked Rajna to translate what I said to the woman. I described some herbs that I thought must grow in such a hot climate, and the woman nodded and went out, returning after a while with the plants. I boiled some and let the infusion trickle into Fatima's mouth. Others I ground up and placed over the wound. I stayed beside her, wiping the sweat that ran in rivers off her forehead.

Rajna told the woman our story, how we had left the ship and then were robbed by our guards, and the woman seemed very sympathetic. She brought us food, and we ate a little. In the afternoon, Fatima began to feel feverish, which worried me, so I asked the woman if there was a doctor nearby. But she told me the only doctors were in the city, and it was far away.

I went out into the yard in front of the house, thinking about what we should do. I looked at the trees that were growing around the yard, and then I found a sort of climbing plant I'd seen in a picture in one of my books. I remembered it perfectly, as it had caught my eye at the time because of its strange shape. I even remembered much of what the book had said, because my mother had made me recite the recipes in the book several times.

I called out, "I found it!"

At the sound of my voice, Rajna came outside and found me tearing off leaves and starting to chew them. I gave some to her and asked her to chew without swallowing, since the plant was poisonous. Then we put the chewed-up leaves over the wound, which had begun to develop a yellow film. Rajna stayed next to Fatima, who swung between wakefulness and sleep. I went outside and sat in the yard, trying to remember if there was anything else I could do to save her. After a while, I felt a hand on my shoulder, and it was Rajna asking me to follow her. When I did, I found Fatima sitting in bed, trying to smile in spite of the pain.

Rajna grabbed my hand. "We did it! Thank God, you're the finest doctor I've ever seen," she said, and she kissed my hand.

I felt Fatima's forehead, and her temperature had gone down a little. She was still in pain, and the place where she'd been bitten looked grim. It was still too early to know whether we'd drawn out all the venom. I was still afraid for her and lay awake all that night. I kept watch over her breathing in case something happened while she slept.

When morning came, she had improved, and even though she didn't want to, we made her eat a little. I felt a great relief that the danger had passed.

The woman who was letting us stay in her home said something to Rajna, then pointed at me.

"She says she has a neighbor whose husband is ill, and she wants you to treat him," Rajna said.

"But I'm not a doctor," I said.

"She says if you can cure a snake bite, then you can help this woman's husband."

"Okay," I agreed. "Tell her to take me to him."

The man was sleeping on a mattress, and at first glance I wondered if he suffered from the same illness as my mother. I tried to ask him whether there was blood coming out when he coughed, and he gestured to me that there wasn't. I felt reassured, and then I examined him carefully, looking particularly at his eyes, as my mother had taught me: "Wherever the illness is in the body, watch the eyes." I indicated that his wife should follow me, and I asked Rajna to translate as I described the herb I wanted to use and scratched its outline in the dust.

Fatima's health was improving, and she was able to go out into the yard with her mother's help, although she still couldn't put weight on her foot, as the pressure caused too much pain in her leg. But color had begun to return to her face.

The woman who boarded us received simple gifts from the villagers in thanks for my services: some brought eggs, some brought a little rice, some brought tobacco. The old woman smoked tobacco out of a long clay pipe that had, at the end of it, a little cup. Our host would fill the cup with tobacco, ignite it, and let the smoke out of her nostrils.

Once Fatima was able to walk well enough, we went on with our journey. We thanked the woman who had hosted us. She looked sorry that we were leaving—perhaps because now the flow of gifts would stop. But, in any case, she gave us a bundle full of food to take with us.

14
A TOUCH OF MAGIC

And so, we continued our journey through the rainforest. We decided to trek through it during the daytime, and as we did, we felt a heightened state of fear. Every time we heard a movement, we froze in place, in terror of a dangerous beast or venomous crawlers. We spoke in whispers. We never stopped to rest and took turns carrying Fatima when she grew tired. We were nearly running, so we didn't notice the shadows deepening. But finally, the trees began to thin, and gradually we started to see the horizon, and we walked toward the setting sun.

Once we'd gotten through the forest, we sat for a while to rest and eat the food the woman had packed for us. Suddenly, we heard behind us the sound of hooves, and in the distance, we saw lamplight and a cart being pulled by two horses. Rajna stood up in front of the horses, startling them.

The cart was of the sort used by farmers to transport their produce, and the old wagoner shouted at her, "Are you mad? You spooked the horses!"

Rajna begged him to take us in his cart to any place beyond the forest, and then she gestured to me to bring Fatima up onto the cart. We climbed into the empty cart, and the man drove on. When I asked Rajna what he'd said, she told me, "He'll put us up for the night in his house."

After a short time, we arrived at a house that was humbler than that of the woman with whom we'd just stayed. The man introduced us to his wife, who welcomed us into the house where the two old people lived alone, then she offered us some food. Rajna translated their conversation.

"He works for the Maharaja of the region. Along with other workers, he takes the farm produce and delivers it to villages—every worker has several villages where he sells the harvest."

Rajna told him a short version of our story and asked if he could bring us to her village. But the old man kindly apologized and said that if the overseer noticed he had taken the wagon, he would tell the Maharaja, who would seize his work and drive him out of his home. Besides, Rajna's village was too far off. So, Rajna replied for us, "Don't worry, and thank you for allowing us to stay overnight and share your food."

Then, I asked him about the Maharaja.

"He's fair, but very strict with his workers," he said. "He has a large palace and a married daughter who lives in the city, and a son who works with him on his many farms. The son is married with several children and lives with his parents in the palace."

"And the Maharaja's wife?"

He looked annoyed.

"That's a different story. She's a demanding and sharp-tongued woman who hates everything except for herself, and she always complains and acts like she's ill to get her husband's attention. Everyone tries to avoid her, even her husband, who spends most of his time traveling, probably to escape from her. She spends all her time sleeping and grooming herself, and, if there's extra time, she spends it torturing her maidservants."

"Anything else?" I asked.

He seemed surprised that I was so interested in the Maharaja's wife.

"I've never seen her myself, and neither have any of the peasants. But everyone passes on stories about her. The Maharani likes parties and showing off in front of her friends—well, not friends so much as freeloaders. You know, my lady, it's said that there's enough food at one of her parties to feed the whole village for a week…People say that she's very stupid, and that the Maharaja married her for her father's money and his vast territories."

"Yes, that's lovely," I said.

Rajna looked at me in surprise.

"What's so lovely about that?"

"God willing, you'll head back to your village in a sumptuous carriage."

"And how's that, when we have only the clothes on our backs?"

I turned to the man.

"Can you take us to the Maharaja's home tomorrow?"

The next day, I tried to freshen up my clothing as best I could, and we went to the Maharaja's house. I told Rajna to ask the maidservant who opened the door to tell her mistress, the grand lady of the palace, that there was an Arab healer at the door who could treat all diseases and make the old become young again.

"Now, you're my assistant," I reminded Rajna, "so do what I ask of you, alright?"

Rajna smiled and gave me a respectful bow.

After a brief wait, the maidservant came back, asking us to enter.

The palace was indescribably luxurious, with ceilings and walls made of carved wood, as well as expensive chandeliers, sumptuous carpets, silk curtains—everything showing off bad taste and enormous wealth. The furniture was luxurious and comfortable, but it was packed into the rooms, suffocating them.

The maidservant led us into a garden that seemed like a piece of paradise. Lush green grass blanketed the earth, and flowers grew everywhere. The smells would have brought a person back from the dead, and the trees surrounding the place were a most glorious green.

The Maharani was lying back against a comfortable armchair as one of the maids gently waved a fan over her head. When I approached, I found she was a woman in her fifties with an overly made-up face, with a lot—*a whole lot*—of gold on her neck and wrists and ears and ankles, which, along with her fleshy body, made me wonder how she could even move.

We approached, and she looked us over carefully, head to toe. Then she settled her gaze on my face, saying something that Rajna translated.

"She asks if you're the Arab healer."

I approached the Maharani with a confidence I didn't really feel and looked at her as a doctor would a patient. Then, I asked Rajna to translate.

"Praise God, I have never in my life seen such a vision of tenderness, beauty, and greatness!"

Rajna struggled to contain herself, and I told her, "Just translate what I say word for word."

When she did, the Maharani smiled broadly and asked me to sit beside her.

"Do you really cure people with herbs and make the old young again?"

"Yes," I said, "although I can see that Your Highness does not need me."

"How don't I need you?"

"Your Highness is still young and in good health—I return youth to the elderly, my lady."

She widened her smile, displaying her teeth.

"She speaks well," the Maharani told Rajna.

"And she lies well," Rajna added as she relayed her words to me.

I urged the lady to continue.

"I have many ailments, and my husband doesn't care about me," she went on. "No one cares about me, or feels my terrible pains, and my husband doesn't bring me doctors. What an ungrateful man! I suffer a lot."

"Is it possible? For such a great and lovely woman to suffer! This isn't right, we must do something."

"Can you help me?" she asked, in a way that made me pity her.

"I'll examine your case, but first I need a few things."

"Ask for anything."

In a commanding tone, I said, "Thieves stole my clothes and belongings. I want to bathe and I want clean clothing. And I want one room for myself, and another for my assistant."

"I'm at your service," she said. "Is there anything else?"

Continuing in the same tone, I instructed, "I will ask for what I need when I need it."

Her maidservant called to another servant, and before going with her, I said to the lady, "After I bathe and rest a little, I will examine your condition."

The two adjoining rooms were the most beautiful and luxurious I'd ever seen, with silken curtains and bedsheets. The maidservant prepared my bath, pouring in hot water and sprinkling rose petals on top. After I'd bathed, I found a pink silk sari on the bed, and Rajna helped me wrap it around my body. She and Fatima both wore new saris, too.

Rajna tucked the folds of the sari around my body.

"What have you done!?" she said softly. "How are we going to get out of this mess? How are you going to bring youth back to this frighteningly unhealthy woman? We'd better flee now before we're found out, and…"

But two servants suddenly entered, carrying trays of food. We ate, and Fatima was the happiest of the three of us. Afterwards, we washed our hands in a copper pot filled with water.

"Let's get to work, my friend," I said to Rajna.

"What will we do now?"

"Make the woman young again," I said. And we laughed.

The Maharani was waiting for us in a spacious room with carpeted floors and walls lined with portraits of men wearing long, colorful turbans. They had long mustaches that reached to their ears.

The lady saw me examining the portraits.

"Those are my ancestors," she said. "I'm descended from an ancient line of Maharajas."

She was sitting on a comfortable armchair, the maidservant again fanning the space above her head.

"I hope the room was to your liking."

"It was fine."

"And will you examine me now?" she asked, hopefully.

With a serious expression, I put my hand over her forehead, then put my hand on her heart, while almost suffocating from her perfume.

"Hmm," I said, in earnest.

"What? What!"

I put my hand on hers, then took her wrist and closed my eyes as I felt her pulse. I asked her to open her mouth so I could look down her throat.

"What?" she asked. "What's wrong with me?"

I told Rajna to instruct her not to speak during the examination.

In truth, I was highly amused by this examination, and even though I was overdoing it, the lady was very patient.

"Now tell me," I said. "What sorts of pains are you having?"

"Ahh, where do I begin? I'm exhausted right away whenever I walk, and my back is continually hurting, and I'm always tired—oh, such a miserable life! Can you help me?"

I spoke seriously and sadly, and Rajna almost couldn't contain herself.

"Regarding your cure, I know what you need, although I don't think I can do it."

"I don't understand...why? You said you could cure anything."

"Yes, my lady, but my treatment is very difficult, and I'm not sure you can follow it."

"Please, the pains will kill me. I'll try."

"I'm a very strict healer, and I like my orders to be followed very carefully."

"I'll follow all your orders. Please."

"It will be hard on you, and it will take some time. And if you don't follow my orders, I'll have to leave the palace."

"I promise," she pleaded.

"And how will you treat this lady?" Rajna said after we left the room. "We're in big trouble now!"

"Listen, my friend, this lady's pains, and everything she complains about, are all on account of overindulgence and boredom. If we can coax her into more activity, her legs will be better able to bear the weight. And, as for the boredom, we'll give her something to occupy her time."

We gave the chef orders to serve the lady only boiled vegetables—without rice, and in small portions—and when the lady saw her food, she cried out in protest.

"What is this slop I'm eating? Bring the cook and I'll punish him!"

"These are my orders," I told her. "Do you object?"

The poor woman said nothing, and she ate her food with annoyance, but in silence.

Next, I began asking her to walk around the garden twice a day—and this was a big garden. On the first day, she protested.

"What is this treatment? You want me to walk all this way? I haven't walked such a distance in all my life!"

I gave her a look that made her say, "Okay, okay, I'll walk, I'll walk."

Before each meal, I gave her an herbal drink to suppress her appetite, and another to strengthen her, and after a while she got used to the smaller portions and she became more able to walk, but her temper grew short and violent.

"If the treatment doesn't suit you," I told her, "then go back to your previous ways. But I won't tolerate your poor treatment and temperament, particularly with the servants."

"But they're servants!"

"They're people. If you're in a bad mood, then go for a walk, but I don't want to see you shouting at the servants."

After a while, she grew more active, and the pain in her legs and back gradually diminished. I began to see the lines of her body emerge. One evening, I told her, "The Maharaja won't know you when he returns from his journey."

She rejoiced.

"Really! Is that true?"

"Of course," I said. "Don't you feel the difference? When we're finished, you'll run like a gazelle."

She clapped her hands together.

"I'll have a big party and invite all my friends—they'll be so jealous of the change in me!"

"Jealous? Tell me, lovely lady, what do you do in your free time, when you're not eating or sleeping?"

"What *can* I do?"

"Well, when was the last time you visited the fields and greeted the farmers?"

"Visit the fields—*me*? Greet the farmers? Are you mad? I'm the daughter of a Maharaja!"

Trying to quell the revolt inside me, I said, "Are you telling me that there's nobody who sees your beauty except your husband and the servants in the palace?"

"My husband doesn't see me!" she said bitterly, and she began to complain about her husband's neglect and lack of interest in her. "He must have mistresses everywhere, the traitor!"

"I'll tell you a story," I said, changing the subject.

"Yes, yes, I love stories."

"There was, in my country, a very rich lady who had money beyond counting, and who was the owner of fields and farmlands farther than the eye could see. This lady was very good—much like you. She cared for both the young and the old, and she visited the farmers in the fields and gave them food with her own hands, and on the holy days she gave them gifts and new clothes."

"What a fool to waste her money on peasants!" the Maharani interrupted.

I flashed her a look that made her shrink back into her place.

"The peasants loved this lady dearly, and when she died, none wept as much as the farmers. And so, many flowers were planted around her tomb that it became a beautiful garden. The peasants visited the tomb every day, and they sang and entertained her, as a tomb is lonely without people. And even though she died many years ago, people still remember her and visit her tomb and call out to her in their prayers to this very day."

"But we don't bury the dead here," she said. "We burn them."

"Ah, but the soul still wanders around, waiting to be reincarnated into a better being, isn't that right?" The lady said nothing, lost in her thoughts. So, I let her contemplate, alone.

The next day, the maidservant called to me, saying that the Maharani was waiting for me in her carriage. And there I found the lady sitting, in all her finery and glory.

"Come on," she said. "Let's visit the fields today. What do you think?"

"That's a lovely idea," I said, amazed.

When we arrived at the fields, the farmers stopped working and looked up at us in bewilderment, as they hadn't seen the lady there before, and most had never even seen her at all. They put their hands near their mouths, under their chins, as a manner of respectful greeting, and they bowed with respect and a little trepidation, as they'd heard about the Maharani's foul temper and feared that her reason for visiting must be a bad one.

The carriage stopped, but she didn't get out. Instead, she stayed in the carriage, waving her hand as royalty do, and the sight was so funny that even Rajna nudged me to look at the expression on her face. Then the lady gestured to her servant to get down, unload the food from the cart behind us, and distribute it to the peasants.

The farmers approached the cart fearfully, and, one by one, they took bundles of food and offered their greetings to the Maharani before they backed away. Then, suddenly, she spoke.

"I'm really tired, and the weather here is so hot, and it's so dusty. Let's go back."

I didn't object, as I didn't want to push too hard on her first visit. So, we went back to the palace. I turned to look behind us, and many of the peasants were watching the carriage with bewildered smiles.

After a while, I learned to understand the language a little. Rajna helped me, and I could practice with her. While I couldn't speak fluently, often I could express myself. One morning, I was walking with the lady in the garden. Her steps had become quicker and her body leaner and stronger. Suddenly, she stopped.

"Oh my goodness! What is today's date?"

"I don't know," I said, and began to think. "It's the seventh of May. My God, the ship!"

"What ship?" she said. "What are you talking about? My husband and son are coming back today, and I have to get ready."

And she hurried back to the palace.

I froze in place, miserable.

I've been here about a month and a half, and I was another ten days in the old woman's house, and two days on the road, oh God! The Jewel must have left for Eden twenty-five days ago! How could I forget?

I called to Rajna.

"It's time to leave! It's too late for me to get the ship back to Eden, but it's been more than a month and a half that we've been living in this palace."

"We're leaving?" she said. "What's the hurry? The ship has left."

"Listen, we can't stay in this palace forever. The Maharaja will be back today, and he might not like finding us here," I said. "I know you're stalling because you're afraid you won't find your family. But you'll have to face it," I added gently.

"You're right," she said. "I have to face my fate sooner or later, and there's no point in delaying any further."

"We'll ask the lady's permission to leave tomorrow. And we'll ask her to provide us a carriage."

"You're coming with me, right?" Rajna asked. "You gave me your word."

"I'm coming with you."

That evening there was complete pandemonium, as the return of the Maharaja and his son caused a great bustle in the palace. I stayed in my room until the maidservant came, requesting our presence, as the Maharaja wanted to see us. As we walked behind the maidservant, I was in a deeply troubled state, not knowing what to expect. We entered a grand dining hall.

We hadn't eaten in this room before, as we ate in the garden with the lady. It was enormous, with a low table at its center, surrounded by luxurious seats. The walls and ceiling were covered in woodcarvings, and it was hung with silk curtains. It wasn't crammed with furniture like the other rooms in the palace, so it seemed more comfortable, and the smell of incense drifted in from somewhere.

The Maharaja was dressed in silks—he had on a golden silk vest. At his breast was a large gold pendant, and in his ears were two large earrings. He wore a turban with neatly arranged feathers, and his huge whiskers touched both ears. His son looked much like him.

With a hand, on which every finger had a golden ring, the Maharaja gestured for us to sit. I took my seat beside his wife, while a flustered Rajna sat at a distance.

"I'm pleased to meet you, my lady," the Maharaja said.

In his language, I replied, "The honor is mine, Lord Maharaja."

"What is this wonder you have wrought with my wife?" he asked, smiling. "I almost didn't recognize her!"

I didn't understand the word *wonder,* and Rajna came up and whispered the meaning into my ear.

"The wonder was wrought by the lady. I didn't do anything,"

I said. And the lady gave a proud smile.

"And how did you convince her to go to the fields? That truly is a wonder!"

"The Maharani is a good woman, and it was she who wanted to help the farmers."

The Maharaja smiled, then gestured that we should start eating.

We ate in silence as the Maharaja exchanged a few words with his son about work. After we'd finished eating, he gestured for the servants to clear away the food and bring us bowls full of warm, perfumed water. Then he said, "I want to speak to this lady alone, so leave us."

The son and the wife rose, but Rajna stayed. He told her to leave as well, turning to me and saying, "You will manage without her."

I sat before him in silence, waiting for him to speak.

"Now," he said, "tell me your story. I understand you appeared all of a sudden at the door to the palace."

And so, in simple words from their language, and with many mistakes, I told him about the ship that sank in the Andalusian Sea, and the caravan, and Eden, and the theft of our possessions.

He listened to me in silence, interrupting only twice to clarify things I didn't express well in my humble sentences.

"That is truly an impressive story."

He was silent for a moment.

"I've been living with my wife for more than thirty years, and this is the first time she's not complaining about anything. This truly is a miracle."

I smiled.

"And now what do you want to do?" he asked. "You can stay here and keep that wild woman busy."

I laughed.

"The Maharani really is good, but she needs a lot of attention.

If my Lord will allow it, I'd like to leave tomorrow. I want to be sure Rajna arrives safely in her village."

"And I can't convince you to change your mind?"

"I found here goodness and generosity. But the time has come, my Lord Maharaja, for me to follow my path."

"Very well. I will prepare a carriage and a guard, and I promise that I'll choose from among my own guards, and they won't steal from you."

I thanked him for his kindness and left.

The next morning, the carriage was ready, loaded with many valuable presents. The lady called on me at the carriage and hugged me until I almost suffocated from her embrace and perfume.

She wept as I told her, "I hope you keep up what we started and don't give up. Otherwise the pain will return."

"I promise, I promise," she said.

The carriage set off, and then suddenly a maidservant came running after us, saying breathlessly, "This is from the Lord Maharaja."

It was a bag of gold coins.

The carriage was pulled by two horses, and we were surrounded by four guards who wore uniforms with the Maharaja's personal emblem, although as for the Maharaja himself, I didn't see him. And so, we drove east toward Rajna's village.

15

THE END OF THE END

When we reached the lands of the Maharaja where Rajna's family lived, I took hold of her hands. They were cold—she was terrified.

"What's the matter?" I asked her. "You've made it home!"

"I don't know what's waiting for me," she explained. "I've been gone for twelve years. I don't know if they're here."

We noticed a woman working at the edge of a field, and she stood up and looked at us. Straightening her back, she studied Rajna's face. Then she raised her hand to her mouth and shouted, "Rajna! Rajna! She's back!" And she started running toward the middle of the field.

We followed slowly behind her in the carriage, and Rajna clung to Fatima as though she were hiding from something, murmuring what must have been a kind of prayer. The woman informed all the farmers she met along the way about Rajna's return, and they stopped working to stare and whisper, "Rajna's back!"

The carriage stopped in the middle of the field. Rajna got down, grabbing Fatima's hand, and looked around. A woman approached and embraced her, pressing her close.

"Rajna's back!" she sighed.

"How are you, Auntie? Are…?" Rajna burst out sobbing and couldn't finish.

"Yes, yes," her aunt reassured her. "They are here."

Soon, a group of people who had recognized Rajna gathered around, glancing at me with curiosity as I stood beside the carriage. An old man emerged from among the group and stood before Rajna. He walked up to her and pressed her to his chest.

"Rajna, my daughter, you're back!"

Rajna dropped to the ground to touch his feet and show respect in the traditional way, but her father lifted her up. Then, her mother came forward. She, too, was very old, and her face was creased with exhaustion, but she ran to Rajna and kissed her fiercely. Rajna sank down to the ground again, kissing her mother's feet, and her mother drew her up and embraced her anew.

Rajna gestured to Fatima, who was standing behind her.

"This is my daughter Fatima, and this is…"

But before she could finish her sentence, the two grandparents engulfed Fatima, hugging and kissing her. Rajna looked at me, apologetically, and I smiled back at her. It wasn't long before her brothers and sisters arrived with their children. It was a moving scene, with everyone—including me—in tears.

Then, from the middle of the crowd, a man called out.

"Go to your houses! You must have a lot to talk about."

He looked at Rajna, and her face reddened when she saw him.

"Welcome back, Rajna," he said.

"But the work…!" her father protested.

"Go, go, we'll do the work," the man said.

He turned to leave, and the rest waved farewell and went with him. We rode in the carriage, together with Rajna's mother and father, and the others walked behind us.

Their house was quite modest. We entered the courtyard, which had an earthen floor. But it was clean, and at its center was a well, just like in the house of the old man who had hosted us and ferried us in his cart. Inside were two rooms and a shed, which served as a kitchen. We sat on seats on the ground, and Rajna, still in disbelief, took my hand and Fatima's, exclaiming, "I'm home, I'm really home!"

When her family had gathered around, she introduced me to them.

"This is my friend Qamar from the Arab lands—she saved my life and Fatima's."

Now, everyone welcomed me, when before they had forgotten about me in all their excitement for their daughter and granddaughter.

"I was afraid I wouldn't find you," Rajna said. "I mean, the son of the Maharaja, he…"

"The Maharaja's son died two days after you left," one of the brothers said. "He fell from his horse. And the Maharaja never knew what had happened between you. If you'd waited a little—"

"If I'd waited a little," Rajna interrupted, "that scoundrel would have raped me, then dropped dead."

"Tell us what's happened to you in all these years," her mother said.

So, Rajna slowly told the story of her escape, her work as a maidservant, and her marriage, laughing and weeping at the same time. She finished with the story of the Maharaja in the western lands, whose wife we had treated. Then, Rajna ran outside to the carriage and came back with several bundles and boxes of the gifts the Maharaja's wife had given us, and she began to hand them out.

In the evening, there was a real celebration, and everyone danced and sang joyfully at Rajna's return. The man who'd met us in the field came, and her face reddened again, making me wonder about their past, and if there was a love story between them.

While Fatima understood the language her mother had taught her, she was still feeling like a stranger, and she clung to me. But the next day, she discovered that she had cousins, both girls and boys her own age, and a little younger. She started playing with them, as any child her age would. I watched from the door as she showed off the scars from her snakebite to the boys and girls.

I stayed with Rajna and Fatima for a week. Then, I told Rajna it was time for me to leave. She asked me where I would go.

"To my country," I said. "The port isn't far from here. I'll find a ship heading for Eden, and from there I'll join a caravan going to Palestine. I think it's time for me to go back to my family, too."

"The port? It will take you too long to sail around the southern tip of India. Why not go west by land to Mumbia?" Rajna asked, puzzled.

"No, my dear, I won't dare provoke fate again."

"I'll never see you again, will I?"

"I'll always be with you," I promised her.

"I suppose there's no point in trying to convince you to stay."

"I'll always carry you and Fatima in my heart."

I shared the money the Maharaja had given us with this good family, as well as with Rajna and Fatima, who was anxious and didn't want me to leave. It was a tearful farewell—how much I hate goodbyes! Why am I always leaving those I love?

Then I set off in the carriage, and, when I looked back, I could see Rajna, Fatima, and her family waving at me. Then I resettled in my seat.

This is a new journey, I thought to myself. *Who knows?*

The trip lasted three days, which passed without difficulties. When I arrived in the large city of Madras, I rented a room in an inn, discharged the carriage and guards, and asked them to bring my grateful thanks to the Maharaja and his wife. Then, I went to my room and lay down on the bed.

Now, I would finally go back to my country. Rajna's return to her family had affected me deeply, and I imagined Shams and her children greeting me. At last I had finished running. Then I thought of Ahmed and Najma, and felt a sharp pang in my heart. *Oh Lord, keep them safe wherever they may be. And, oh Lord, forgive me. I am tired of searching.*

The next morning, I asked about ships and learned that one was leaving for Eden in three days' time! So, I reserved a cabin, paid the captain the fare, then went back to get to know the city.

Madras was big and beautiful, full of markets with goods beyond reckoning. It reminded me a lot of Tangier, and in two days I got to know a slice of it. On the third day, as I went to board the ship, I caught a glimpse of the figurehead on the ship's prow—a giant carved wooden nymph with the body of a fish and the head of a beautiful woman, her hair covering her chest. She was so perfectly magnificent that it seemed she was about to escape from the front of the ship into the sea.

I must have stood before her for a long time, because I heard the sailors call out, "Travelers up top! Travelers up top! The ship's ready to sail!" So I quickly climbed the swinging stairs to the top, and soon after, the sailors lifted anchor, untied the ropes, and the ship began to sail. I stood to the side and looked back at the harbor.

"Farewell Rajna, farewell Fatima," I whispered. "I wish you a happy life."

Then, I went to my cabin, laid on my bed, and dozed off.

I awoke to the sound of a knock at the door. I opened it and a woman stood there.

"Her Royal Highness, the Princess, invites you to dine at her table this evening. Please do not be late."

I was still half-asleep.

"The Princess? What Princess?"

"Her Royal Highness, Princess Hatta, the Princess of the Island of Ceylon, is on board ship. She invites you to join her table at dinner."

"Thank the Princess, and tell her I will be honored to dine at her table."

I bathed and began to change my clothes. It was fortunate that I'd found a shop in Madras where I could buy clothes like the ones I usually wore. I was very happy, because even though I'd been in India for several months, I hadn't gotten used to or mastered the sari, despite all of Rajna's efforts to teach me. So I got back into my Arab clothing, climbed up the stairs to the deck, and asked the first sailor I saw if he knew where to find the Princess's cabin. He pointed to where I'd just come from, and I went back down the stairs again and found it not far from my own room.

I knocked on the door, and the same woman opened it and admitted me. In truth, her room was nothing like mine— it was wide and had a comfortable bed in it. I felt as though I were in a room of a real palace!

The Princess spoke in Hindi, although with a strong accent.

"Welcome, and thank you for accepting my invitation. Please, have a seat."

I took the seat to which she'd pointed. She was a woman in her early thirties, a bit younger than me, both beautiful and magnificent. She studied me closely.

"You must have been surprised by my invitation!" she said.

"In truth…" I said.

"I do not like to eat alone," she continued. "So I asked the captain if there were any honorable ladies on board ship, and he suggested that I ask you."

"It is an honor, my lady," I said politely.

"Now, we will eat," she said. "Then we'll talk."

She clapped her hands, and servants entered in silence to lay the dishes on the silver table before us. We began to eat, and during the meal the Princess spoke about Madras and its beauty, its shops, and other things, while I listened agreeably, as a guest does.

Once we'd finished, the servants cleared the dishes and brought in two ewers of water and perfumed napkins. Then they reappeared, bringing with them an assortment of fruit, which they set out on the table. After that, they left.

The only attendant who remained was the woman who had opened the door for me, and she sat by the Princess's feet like a cat awaiting a signal. Her posture reminded me of Mawahib, the slave of Noor al-Huda.

The Princess turned to me. "Now tell me about yourself."

I avoided responding directly.

"In truth, there's not much to say."

"Come," she said cheerfully. "Every person has a story, and every life makes a tale."

"I don't know what to tell you, my lady. I'm traveling from Madras to Eden."

"That's a good start," she said. "It's clear from your attire that you're Arab. So what's an Arab woman doing traveling alone? Come, come, there must be an amusing story, and I love stories!"

So, I told her about Rajna and our trip, and when I told her about the wife of the Maharaja, she laughed so much that her servant had to pour her a glass of water.

"That was a very entertaining story," she said. "Do you really know about herbal medicine? Or was it just a trick to convince the wife of the Maharaja?"

"Yes," I said, worrying about what I was getting myself into. "I do know a bit about herbs."

She reflected for a moment, as though seeing me in a different way.

"How did you learn?"

"From books."

"Do you read?" she asked, surprised.

"Yes."

"That's lovely. My father tried to teach me to read, but I was lazy and grew bored quickly, so he washed his hands of me. My husband passes many hours reading."

Then she grew serious.

"Can you heal all illnesses with herbal medicine?"

"Not all," I said. "There are many illnesses that can't be treated—with herbs or otherwise."

Her expression grew intent.

"Such as?"

"I mean, there are many common ailments that can be treated with herbs. And there are some for which we don't yet have treatments. I'm not—"

"Infertility," she cut in. "Can you treat infertility?"

"Infertility? I'm not sure… I've heard of an herb that helps with such conditions, but I have never tried to find it, nor to test it. I remember seeing it in one of the books—"

"What is it?" she asked eagerly. "What's it called? Where's it found?"

"My lady," I said, "I can't remember at the moment. It's been a long time, and I…"

"Come on, *remember.*"

Then she noticed the sharpness of her tone, which was more imperious than necessary.

"I mean, can you remember?"

I looked at her beautiful face, which was worried and

miserable, and yet her eyes sparkled with hope. *Good God, what have I gotten myself into now?* I wondered.

"How long have you been married, my lady?" I asked her.

"For almost fourteen years. I've been trying to have a child…"

She surrendered herself to tears. Then she pulled herself back together.

"Do you know how much it hurts not to have a child to play and laugh with? Why can't I have a baby like other women? Why is it possible for them and forbidden to me? I want just one child, someone to call me Mama."

And I cried too, remembering Najma, her joy and her laughter, and the hugs from her two small arms. "But being a mother can bring other heartaches," I said. "Like having a child to play and laugh with, and call you Mama, and then losing her…"

The Princess handed me a glass of water. I was still crying and wiping away my tears, and couldn't force myself to stop. After a long silence, she spoke to me sympathetically.

"You've had a tragedy in your life. Tell me…"

So, I told her about Ahmed and Najma, and how I'd lost them, and we both wept. After a while, I said, "My lady, I'd like to go back to my cabin."

"Go on," she said. "But please—in your daughter's name—help me and remember those herbs."

I agreed to try, and went back to my cabin.

I spent the next day with Princess Hatta, whose company I enjoyed. She told me about her life, and her marriage to Prince Bihan, who was loyal to her and didn't marry another.

"He's begun to look gloomy, and he must wonder who will inherit the throne after him, as I cannot give him a child."

"But there are many women who don't give birth," I told her. "It isn't the end of the world."

"It's the end of the world for me," she said sharply. "You are my life's last hope. I've been trying to have children since I got married fourteen years ago. It's too much for me."

"That's a big responsibility," I said. "It may be more than I can do."

I became a permanent guest at the Princess's table, and we talked about everything. Yet the conversation would always turn back to the subject of herbal medicine.

On the fourth day of our voyage, she said, "Tomorrow, the ship will dock at our island. Come with me—my husband has a large library in the palace, and you may find a book that helps you remember the herbs." She continued, imploring, "Come with me. If you help me, I'll order a special ship to take you to Eden." Then she gave a sad sigh. "You don't know how much I love my husband and how much I want to give him a child."

"I can imagine, my lady," I said, handing myself over to the will of God.

"I will give you more jewels and money than you've ever seen."

"My lady, if I help you, it is because you've become my friend, not for jewelry or money."

"I apologize, I didn't mean to offend. But you're my last hope."

On the fifth day, we arrived at her island, and, as the ship neared the port, the Princess took my hand.

"That's my husband, there. Do you see him? He's wearing a green turban. Isn't he handsome? I still feel a quiver in my heart whenever I see him."

And she began to wave her handkerchief at him.

We went down to the shore, where she greeted him warmly. Then she introduced me.

"This is my friend Qamar, from the Arab lands, and she'll be our guest for some time."

"Ahlan wa sahlan fi gazeeratina—welcome to our island," the Prince said to me in good Arabic.

I was surprised, and the Princess smiled at me.

The Prince laughed and lovingly took her hand, leading her to the carriage. Then he bowed to me again and said, "After you, Sayyidati."

The carriage set off, and, along the way, the Princess told her husband about her trip to Madras and how she'd met me. When we arrived at the palace, the Princess approached the servants who were lined up in front of the entrance. She gave greetings to some and orders to others, and a maidservant came to show me to my room.

I was still contemplating the room's beautiful furniture when there was a knock on the door, and two servants entered with my luggage. I rested a little and changed my clothes. Then a maidservant came to call me to dine at the Prince and Princess's table.

The Princess, relieved of the burdens of travel, was radiant, and she was cooing at her husband in a loving way. Prince Bihan truly was as handsome as the Princess had said. He turned and directed his words at me.

"My wife has told me a little about you—you must have had some interesting experiences in your life."

"I can't call it interesting, although I've surely had enough troubles for three more lives."

Sensing that I didn't want to dwell on the subject, he asked, "Are you truly adept with herbal medicine?"

"A little," I said. "Although I need to refresh my memory."

"My library is at your service. You may use it whenever you wish."

"If the question is not too forward, how did you learn to speak Arabic, and so well?"

"It isn't too forward, Sayyidati, not at all. My father was

a great lover of the sciences and reading. As I grew, he taught me, and then he sent me to Baghdad. There, I spent five years in my studies, because your lands are the center of science and knowledge. I returned to my country laden with books. But what country are you from?"

"From Palestine," I said. "Where Jerusalem is found."

"Ah, Jerusalem!" he said. "I've heard so much about it."

The conversation moved from one topic to another, and we would speak a bit in Arabic and then translate what we said into Hindi. But then I noticed that the Princess began to look distressed.

"It's better for us to speak Hindi, so the Princess doesn't feel bored," I told the Prince.

The next morning, I went to the library, which truly was quite large, and I began by looking through the Arabic books. All the books were classified precisely, with each language occupying a place, and each subject written in that language in its particular place. I examined and flipped through many of them, searching for ones about herbs and healing. I realized that I had read some of them before, which made me feel homesick for those times when I'd lived quietly among my family's books.

Then, I came upon a high shelf with a book bound in red. My heart began to beat quickly… Could it be? I reached up and grasped the book…and it was *the* book—*Wondrous Journeys*. I couldn't believe it! This book, the companion of all my journeys, had been lost at sea when the ship went down. I flipped through its pages, smiling and crying at the same time, as if I'd come across an old friend.

Then I heard a gentle cough, and turned to find the Prince sitting in one of the chairs and looking at me with a smile.

"I hadn't notice you come in, my lord."

"No reason to worry," he responded. "Have you found

something?" he asked, looking at the book of wonders in my hand.

"It's a dear book, and I lost my copy when…"

"I mean about herbs."

"I have an herb in mind, but I can't remember its name. I'm still looking… You have a wonderful library here!" I said, trying to ease the awkwardness of the situation.

"Yes, my father and I spent many long years collecting these books."

He pointed to the book *Wondrous Journeys.*

"I bought that from a bookshop in Baghdad, and the copyist told me he'd made only five copies."

"In truth, I have a long history with this book."

"I have time, and you'll find me a good listener. Shall we walk in the gardens?"

Before we walked, he smiled and pointed to his nose, but I didn't understand.

"Your nose is dirty," he said matter-of-factly.

I wiped at my nose with a handkerchief, and my face reddened.

"It's the ink. After a time, the ink becomes…"

"It's nothing. Shall we walk?"

"Where's the Princess?"

"Resting."

We started to walk in the garden and the Prince wanted to know the story of my relationship with this book.

"Is Your Highness prepared for a long story?"

"You'll find I'm all ears."

I began from the beginning, in my family's village, and went on until I reached the part where I met Princess Hatta.

"And the rest you know, my lord," I said, finishing.

The Prince remained silent for a time.

"My God, all this?" he finally responded. "I don't know what to say except that I hope, with all my heart, that you can find comfort and peace."

We talked about many things, about the Arabs and their sciences, about books, and we talked like old friends without noticing the passage of time until a maidservant came hurrying up.

"Her Highness invites you to come dine," she informed us.

The Princess was waiting for us in the dining room with an angry look, and the Prince said fondly, "Whoever has angered the Prince's beloved, I'll cut off his head."

She gave a sulky smile.

"Could the Prince cut off his own head? You left me alone all morning!"

"I'm sorry, I apologize. We got caught up in our talk and didn't notice. Do you forgive me?"

He kissed her hand.

"Very well," she said, "I'll forgive you this time."

But the Prince began to spend more time with me. He would come to the library wanting to spend hours talking about everything. It wasn't long before the Princess started to erupt with anger, sometimes refusing to eat. I told the Prince I could appreciate that the Princess's anger was sparked by jealousy.

"It's best we don't meet and talk so much, as it upsets her."

"She knows that I love her, and that I'll never leave her," he said. "And I'm so excited to talk to a woman as miraculous as you. Frankly, I've started to be annoyed by her jealousy."

So, I tried to keep clear of the Prince. I would go to the library only to take a few books and read them in my room. I avoided being alone with him and would claim I was ill every time he sent a maidservant to ask about me.

Finally, I found the herb I was looking for clearly drawn on a page in one of the books, and I discovered its name and location. I ran to the Princess and said with joy as I opened the book, "I found it, I found the herb, and I think it should be easy to get it. Look!"

The Princess gave the book a cold look.

"Good. I'll ask my doctor to bring it."

Now that I had completed my mission, I had to get out of this place. It was clear that the Princess no longer welcomed me, believing I had a special relationship with her husband, beyond the friendship of two bibliophiles. She went on treating me coldly, so to avoid the situation I spent long hours in my room, pretending to be tired.

That morning, I found a ship that would stop at the island the next day and continue on to Eden. Later, the Princess's maidservant came to me and told me that the Princess would like to walk with me in the city.

"It would be an honor," I said. "Tell the Princess I'm very happy that she's feeling better."

I decided to take the opportunity to tell the Princess about my intention to leave the next day. When the Princess stepped out of her room, she looked radiant, having regained her vitality and joy. I thought it must be because she'd finally realized I had neither betrayed nor harmed her, and I was relieved.

"I'm so glad to see you're happy and well again—I missed you very much."

Cheerfully, she took my hand. "Let's go walk a bit in town."

We rode in the carriage, and the Princess chattered the whole way. Telling me about everything we passed, she left me no room to let her know about my decision to depart. She went on chattering about endless topics, as if she wanted to make up for all that we'd missed talking about for the past two weeks.

We arrived at a market full of shops, and it was smaller than the one in Madras, although cleaner and better organized. The market was full of many beautiful things, and each had its own section—there was even a corner just for the fish vendors, who weren't allowed to sell their fish elsewhere. It was the same for sellers of vegetables, fabrics, and spices.

"It was my idea to organize the market this way," the Princess said. "Isn't it fantastic? In the past, when I used to buy silk, it smelled of fish. Isn't this so much better?"

She talked and talked, and then we stopped in front of a fabric shop. She turned to her maidservant, who'd been walking behind us, and signaled to her quietly with a hand, as if I wasn't paying attention. It made me wonder if perhaps she wanted the maidservant to buy some silks for me as a surprise. We went on walking, with the maidservant behind us, and the Princess continued chattering and pointing to things, telling me their names.

Suddenly, a woman appeared in front of us. She was wearing dirty clothes, and her skin was completely covered. She approached me, her face and body cloaked, and said something that I didn't understand. Then she lunged forward, uncovered her face, and pressed it to mine. I pushed her off me forcefully. She stepped back and covered her face again, and as she did, I noticed that her hand and her face were covered in white sores and that one of her fingers was missing. Then the woman disappeared into the marketplace as quickly as she'd appeared.

I wiped my face with my handkerchief and turned to the Princess.

"What was that about?"

"A beggar woman, pay no attention. I'm sorry she bothered you."

I continued wiping my face.

"I'm fine, but she surprised me! Is that how people ask for charity in your country?"

"No, no, never," she said. "Her behavior was very strange. I'm sorry, should we go back to the palace?"

On our way back, the maidservant rode with us in the carriage. The Princess had stopped chattering and was giving only brief replies, as if she'd lost her desire to speak. I thought perhaps she was embarrassed at the behavior of the strange woman. I decided this was the right time to tell her about my departing.

"There's a ship that will pass by here tomorrow on its way to Eden. I've decided to leave on it and head back to my country."

The Princess gasped and clapped a hand to her mouth, then looked at the maidservant who was sitting beside her, listening. I assumed that she grieved at the idea of our separation.

"Please don't be sad. I've missed my country, and I only ever intended to stay here a short while."

The Princess began to cry, and I reached out my hand to take hers, but she yanked it back quickly, surprising me.

"Please don't be angry with me," I pleaded.

"I'm sad you're leaving," she said.

Then we were all silent until we reached the palace.

In the evening, she sent a sumptuous dinner to my room, and I didn't see her for the rest of the day. When I asked her maidservant, she said that her lady was tired and begged my pardon.

In the morning, the servants carried my luggage to the carriage along with several other boxes, possibly gifts from the Princess. When I arrived at the carriage, the first light of day had just begun to shine, and I saw Prince Bihan standing beside the carriage.

"Would you allow me to take you to the ship?"

"I'd be honored, Your Highness, but where is the Princess? I want to take my leave."

"She was exhausted yesterday and didn't sleep well, so I left her sleeping." He added, "I'm sure she would have loved to say her farewells, but she was very tired."

I accepted his lie and entered the carriage. Before we arrived at the port, he gave me something wrapped in silk, saying, "Please accept this gift from me."

I opened it, found the book *Wondrous Journeys,* and smiled gratefully.

The Prince saw me off warmly.

"If the winds ever bring you back to our country, remember you will always be welcome."

I thanked him and went up to the ship, and I remained standing there on the deck until we moved off. Then I went to my cabin and lay on the bed, thinking about the Princess's strange behavior. I tried to understand why she had changed so suddenly when we were at the market, why her scowls had returned, and why she hadn't come to see me off.

In those first days of the voyage, I felt no desire to climb up on deck, and nothing really interested me. After that, I began to feel tired, and I could find no reason for it. I thought maybe I'd come down with a cold, and I forced myself to take some herbs to the ship's kitchen and boil them. When I got back to my room, I was very tired. After I'd drunk the herbal infusion, I lay down and tried to sleep, telling myself that when I woke, I'd feel better.

Two weeks passed with me locked up in that room, as fever and fatigue had begun to wrack my body, and chills and pains besieged my joints and organs. I thought it was only a fever, and would pass, until I woke one morning to a severe, squeezing pain in my joints. I looked at my hand and saw some strange spots.

I thought about all the diseases that displayed symptoms like this: colorless patches that were white at the edges, and suddenly I remembered the woman at the market. My God, it was leprosy! I started searching my memory to confirm or deny the diagnosis, and all the symptoms confirmed that it was so.

The story that I put together was shocking: the Princess had arranged for me to meet this woman with leprosy so I'd get infected and she'd be rid of me! No, this couldn't be! But I remembered in minute detail—how she'd snatched her hand away from mine when we were on our way back, and how she'd disappeared and I didn't see her again after our trip to the market. How she didn't come say goodbye. My God! Could a person stoop so low? Had she reached such a pitch of jealousy that she had to get rid of me in this hideous way? She could have driven me off, or poisoned my food, or… But this! Could a person's hatred go so far? What a wretched revenge!

What can I do now? By the time I reach Eden, the leprosy could spread all over my body, and people will avoid me or run from me—no one will come near me! What should I do?

I kept thinking as I wept fiercely. *The worst of it is that no caravan leader will be allowed to bring a woman with leprosy, and I'll never get to Palestine. If the captain of this ship were to find out, he'd throw me into the sea for fear I'd spread the disease to the rest of the passengers.*

I packed up my belongings and sent a note to the captain that I'd like to be set down at the first island at which he stopped.

Passing through a beautiful chain of islands, the Maldives, the ship entered port at one.

I stood on the beach holding my luggage. As the ship moved away, it took with it all hope of me ever returning to my country. It was the end of the end.

16
A PATH TOWARD LIFE

I bought a small house overlooking the sea, where I settled myself, intending to spend the rest of my life there. I would sit on the balcony or walk down the beach, thinking about all my adventures and all that had been lost to me. That's when I decided to commit my memories and journeys to paper. Perhaps it was to relieve my loneliness, or because I wanted to bring everything back so I could live it again, moment by moment. And so, I began to write.

I wrote quickly, hurrying to finish before I lost my hands to leprosy. But three months later, I was surprised to find that the disease hadn't spread. What I had taken for signs of the disease began to disappear; the spots faded from my hands. Had I misdiagnosed myself? Was the illness borne of my horrible imaginings? Or, was the air of this peaceful island giving me an illusion of recovery?

Whatever the reason, my symptoms gradually diminished, until I could say I was almost completely recovered. Had I wasted my time in withdrawing here? Could I now continue my journey to Eden? I decided to wait a little longer and observe my condition.

After six months hidden away on this island, I recovered completely. I was restored to my former state of health, without any apparent trace of the disease. So, it hadn't been leprosy, but something else—and now it was gone! I could finally continue on to Eden.

I went to the port to inquire about ships. There, they told me they didn't know exactly when ships would arrive, as one might anchor for a day to restock food and water, then leave just as suddenly. So, I offered a boy I used to see playing on the shore some money, promising to give him more if he would come tell me right away when an Eden-bound ship had moored. Then, I went back to my house, gathered up my things, and waited.

The wait was difficult, as I had to be ready to leave at any moment, and I knew might have to wait for a day, a month, or more. But three weeks later, I spotted the boy running toward the house, waving both arms at me. We grabbed my luggage and headed to the port, where indeed I found a ship bound for Eden.

Once on board, I kept writing—mostly to stop myself from thinking about how, when I got to Eden, I would join the first caravan headed for Palestine. Did fate once again have something in store for me? *Oh, Fate, test someone else. I no longer have the energy for your surprises!*

When I arrived in Eden, I kissed the ground. At last, an end to my adventures. I found my way to the khan where I'd met Anfara a few months back and asked about him. The keeper informed me that his ship would arrive in three days. So, I went to my room, where I fell into a deep sleep until the next morning.

I woke up feeling rested and went downstairs to ask the keeper if there would soon be a caravan headed for Palestine. He said that in three weeks one would be heading out on pilgrimage to Mecca, and from there I could join another, bound for Palestine.

My God, pilgrimage time again! It had been more than a year since the *Conqueror of the Sea* had been lost at sea. The painful ache returned, which I felt whenever I thought of Ahmed and Najma.

I decided to go out for a walk around the city, but when I was leaving the khan, my eyes were still full of tears that I had to wipe with a handkerchief. I paid so little attention to another traveler entering the front door that I knocked into him.

"Qamar!" a familiar, beloved voice exclaimed.

I looked at him and, for a moment, my heart stopped. The world began to spin, and I fell unconscious from the shock.

I woke to find myself stretched out on my bed, with Ahmed gazing at me lovingly. I closed my eyes again.

Such a dream! I don't want to wake up. I want to see Ahmed again. But something inside me told me this was real, and I heard his warm, tender voice and felt the touch of his hand on my forehead.

"Qamar, Qamar."

I opened my eyes and saw that it *was* him—Ahmed, in the flesh and blood. I grabbed hold of him and held him tightly, and still I couldn't believe it. It wasn't possible! I couldn't let go of him for fear he'd leave me and be lost once again, and we held each other, both of us crying.

"But how did you find me?" I asked him. "When? And Najma, where's Najma? Tell me!"

"Rest a moment and let me look at you—I've missed you and longed for you so much."

He wiped my eyes and took my hand.

"When you didn't come back during the storm, Najmat al-Sabah and I tried to go up onto the deck to search for you. The ship was listing wildly, tilting all the way over, and I realized it

239

would sink. So, I grabbed Najma and latched her hands and feet to a piece of wood so she wouldn't be thrown into the sea. I called out to you, but you didn't answer. Then I spotted you, lying still, beside a crate. I tied you to the wooden mast and tried to revive you. But Najma screamed, and I had to try to get back to her. Everything went by so fast…I don't know what happened next, but something threw me into the water.

"When I woke, I found myself on a beach, not knowing where I was, and not able to remember anything.

"Who was I? How did I end up on that beach? I tried to remember, but my head was full of fog. Then, some of the fishermen helped me, and so I stayed to work with them, not remembering anything about my previous life, my past, or where I'd come from. I couldn't even remember my name, and so the fishermen gave me one. I stayed with them, as one of them, living a new life without a past.

"But as time went on, images began to flash inside my mind—of a girl playing on a beach, a woman reading a book on a balcony, images like dreams. They increased, but they were confusing and unclear, as though behind a curtain. They would come to me suddenly and then disappear. I was sure they had something to do with my past, but I couldn't piece them together.

"Then I began to have nightmares. I'd see a ship sinking in a raging sea, people crying out for help, and a child screaming, 'Baba, Baba!'

"One morning, I woke up to the horrible truth…I remembered everything, all at once—the ship, Najma, you— and I was gripped by fear. I didn't know your fate, whether you'd gone down with the ship or survived. I started asking around to find out about the ship, but nobody knew anything. So, I decided to go back to Tangier, where I heard the *Conqueror of the Sea* had sunk, and where there might be some survivors.

"I went to the house with the unshakeable hope of finding you and Najma there. And the servants told me that *you* had joined a caravan headed for Egypt, looking for *us*! Then, when I returned to Tangier, I came across my old friend Zein al-Deen —do you remember him?—who told me that you'd ridden with the caravan, but changed course and headed to Eden. So, I came here to Eden and asked about you in all the city's khans, until I reached this one. The owner told me you came here about a year ago, and that you met a merchant named Abdullah and traveled with him to India. I've been waiting here…to ask him about you."

When Ahmed finished his story, both of us wept.

"And Najma?" I asked. "Do you know what's happened to her? Could she have drowned? I don't believe it! Ahmed, we have to find our daughter."

"We will look for her, and we'll find her, God willing."

I held onto him, crying, not believing he was actually here and that he was still alive. I laughed, then cried, then laughed, and I still couldn't believe he was really here.

"I can't believe I'm really seeing you…What if I had been delayed on that island? What if I hadn't met you?"

"I'm here," he said, laughing. "Let's not think about that now. Tell me what happened to you."

And so, I told him about everything that had happened to me, from the moment I found myself floating on that piece of wood at sea.

How I'd gone to our house and rode with a caravan first to Egypt, and then to Abyssinia, then to Eden. I told him about meeting Anfara, about India and Rajna and Fatima, the elephant, about the wife of the Maharaja and the Princess of Ceylon, and about my fear of the disease that I thought was leprosy, and my return to Eden.

We spent the next two days thinking and talking about where to start the search for our daughter, as finding one another had reignited our hopes that she might still be alive. Then, we heard a knock at the door. Ahmed opened it, and there was a boy who worked at the khan.

"Mr. Abdullah asks permission to see the lady in the reception hall of the khan."

We went downstairs and found Anfara.

"Abdullah, this is my husband," I told him, smiling. "I found him!" The two men greeted each other heartily, having met each other through me.

After a warm exchange, Anfara asked, "Now tell me what happened to you. I waited three days and couldn't postpone the trip any longer. The winds would have changed."

So, I told him all that happened in India, and he said, "Thank God you're safe. And now, have you had enough adventures?" Then suddenly he smacked his forehead. "My God, I almost forgot. I heard that some of the children from the slave caravan didn't reach Eden and were sold in Abyssinia. It's said that the man who bought them is a tribal chief there."

My heart thundered, and I seized Ahmed's hand and squeezed it hard.

"Najma."

Ahmed squeezed back.

"Then we'll go to Abyssinia."

"I'll take you there myself," Anfara said, and he left immediately to make arrangements.

That evening, he returned.

"Everything's ready! We leave tomorrow morning. A small ship is waiting for us."

"So fast!" Ahmed exclaimed gratefully. "You are a gallant man!"

Then Ahmed turned to me. "We'll leave no stone unturned.

If she's alive, we'll find her, God willing."

"And this is for you, Sayyidati," Anfara said, handing me a bundle. "What is it?" I asked.

"Clothes," he said, smiling.

"Thanks, but I don't understand."

"Open it."

I opened it and found—men's clothing!

"This time, you'll travel as a man. We don't want you to be kidnapped." He turned to Ahmed. "We don't want to find one only to lose the other."

In the morning, I put on the men's clothes and sheathed a sword in my belt. They felt strange yet familiar . "What do you think?" I asked Ahmed.

He laughed. "Now I know what you looked like as a pirate. But how did they fail to notice such beauty? And does my lord the pirate give us permission to rob a ship while we're on our way?"

We went downstairs to find Anfara, who was waiting for us.

"Good morning, Mr. Ahmed," he said. "And good morning, Mr. Ajeeb."

Then, we went down to the dock, where we found Hamid from *The Black Angel* waiting for us. He looked at me with a big smile.

"How could I miss an adventure like this?" he asked.

It's hard to describe the happiness I felt as I stood beside Ahmed. I couldn't believe he was alive and traveling with me. *Oh God, will you complete my happiness?*

The water was calm, and the ship cut through it like a sharp knife through butter. It was dawn, the sky was clear, and I could clearly see the stars above me, one by one. It was as though, if I reached out a hand, I could pluck one from the sky.

The morning star was shining, beckoning me towards it. The star I had named my daughter after.

The ship glided quietly, and a calm came over me, such as I hadn't felt in a long time. On the watery surface, I could see my life clearly written, each stroke of the oars another page of my life. How many pages, how many beats of my heart, had already passed before me?

I could see myself as a three-year-old girl, climbing an olive tree, and the ghosts of the village passing in front of me without noticing my presence; then as a girl of eight, my fingers stained with ink, trying to draw, the letters swaying in harmony over the blank page. I could see my mother sitting in front of me, reading a book, a satisfied smile on her face. And my father, sweaty, plowing our small patch of land, his expression filled with contentment.

I could again see Aisha, our family's helper, combing my hair and humming a wordless song; two graves entwined together beneath a tree, and a group of village women arriving silently, lighting a lamp, and then departing in silence.

With another stroke of the oars, I could see the days passing, brightened by my sister Shams' smile, her hand waving at me as tears washed over her face, and feel again the first shock of surprise at the sun glinting off the Dome of the Rock in Jerusalem. I could see the dear face of Umm Najmuddin, always worried; Noor al-Huda lifting her feet and leaping gracefully onto a horse; the sad look of my teacher in Tangier, heartbroken as I gathered my books and luggage to venture off into an unknown future.

I smiled at Alaa al-Deen's face painted clearly on the water, winking at me: "Isn't life one big adventure?"

The faces of my friends—Monkey, Anfara, Abdoun, Cabbage—passing in front of me. How many caravans, ships, oceans, deserts and travels!

Zein al-Deen, Rajna, Fatima, the Maharani, Princess Hatta, Um Saad—so many beloved faces! Whether far away or dead, they left a spot of light in my heart.

I saw Ahmed, my husband and friend, walking with me on the beach and comforting me with his wisdom. "Peace doesn't mean death. Peace is another kind of adventure, when things in life intertwine toward growth."

My sweet child Najmat al-Sabah, whose laughter was so pure when her feet touched the cold water of the sea, who raced with the foam of the waves as they moved in and out, and who never tired of wrangling with them.

And yet, here I was in the heart of the world, sailing off once more. This would be my final adventure. But not to discover the unknown or to indulge a craving that long pushed me to head down mysterious roads. This time, the way ahead no longer looked hazy. This time, at the end of the path I could see my family, together again. This time I could see the three of us—reunited, and heading together toward the greatest adventure of all—life.